THE CURSED

MICHAEL PANCKRIDGE

THE CURSED

YOU CAN'T FIGHT WHAT YOU CAN'T SEE

MICHAEL PANCKRIDGE

First published in 2007 by

black dog books

15 Gertrude Street
Fitzroy Vic 3065
Australia
+61 3 9419 9406
+61 3 9419 1214 (fax)
dog@bdb.com.au
www.bdb.com.au

Designed by Blue Boat Design
Cover design by Ektavo Pty Ltd
Printed and bound in China by 1010 Printing International
Cover photographs: Shutterstock

Every effort has been made to trace and acknowledge copyright material. The author and publisher would be pleased to hear from any copyright holders who have not been acknowledged.

Panckridge, Michael, 1962- .
The Cursed.

For children.
ISBN 9781742031453

10 9 8 7 6 5 4 3 2 1   10 11 12 13

To Jo, Eliza and Bronte

who kept believing as

Mapute turned into

the *Invisible Boy*

and finally became

The Cursed

CONTENTS

PROLOGUE

FILE NO: 675653 THE LIGHT CRUSADERS
— (ORIGIN LEIGHT)

In the late 1750s (some historians put the date a decade or so earlier) a secret society was formed by John Leight — a popular and respected publican in a town called Fenwick. Fenwick was one of the pottery towns of Derbyshire in England and the secret of making fine china had brought great wealth to some members of the community. But with wealth came crime.

Returning to the inn late one night, Leight had been set upon by a band of thugs and his purse, with all the inn's takings, had been stolen from him. Tired of the sin around him, John resolved to take matters into his own hands.

He invited twelve men to his inn. They were twelve men of honor, strength of character and courage — men held in high esteem by the townsfolk. There he explained his vision. It was John Leight's belief that the authorities of the town were weak and corrupt — unwilling and unable to stop crime. The parish constables and 'watch' systems in place were effectively nonexistent. John and his twelve colleagues would develop their own ways of eliminating sin from the town, and secrecy was their key.

The group of thirteen called themselves The Leight Crusaders of Fenwick. They would meet monthly and plan their shadowy missions. To help fellow members identify each other, and also ensure that Crusaders wouldn't be identified when carrying out their work (thus protecting their families), John Leight made every Crusader a mask.

These masks, close-fitting and made of a pale white ivory, quickly became the symbol of The Leight. They represented the anonymous nature of a Leight Crusader.

The society's work began slowly at first and always in secret, but whispers and rumors spread. Rogues and vagabonds came to hear of special meetings of The Leight Crusaders of Fenwick, or simply The Leight as it came to be called. Thieves would find that they were not alone in the dark of night. Forgers would suddenly find themselves a victim of forgery. Some criminals simply disappeared. Others soon went elsewhere. But so did John Leight's movement. Town by town, across the breadth of England, groups were formed and the movement grew. Every month saw a new chapter of The Leight Crusaders formed in a new town.

One of the few documents to have survived on the public record from the founding group in Fenwick was a declaration penned by John Leight himself that espouses the values of the group.

At certain times it behoves on one individual to stand up and in front of his fellow kind declare to the world that every person has the right to equality, liberty, peace and prosperity. Furthermore, in the eyes of God himself, that individual must stand tall and gather round him men of strength, good character, sound reason and clear mind to remove from our world all those parasites, heathens, villains and ne'er do wells who threaten to compromise our rights.

That time is now, and that man is I.

I hereby declare that the fight for justice and peace has begun and furthermore that it shall not cease until the battle for equality, liberty, peace and prosperity is fought and won.

Within twenty years, the movement crossed the English Channel and spread into Europe. The people were happy. Criminals, thieves, murderers, and scurrilous men in business were being removed. Taken away. No one knew exactly where to and no one asked. It was enough that they were gone. The authorities were content. It seemed that only the wrongdoers were suffering.

The movement became known as The Light — in honour of John Leight, its founder, the 'e' being dropped to give a broader meaning to the movement.

The organization spread to the United States and other English-speaking countries during the early 1800s and from there to other parts of the world. The Light was taken into South America by Yankee traders after the end of the American Civil War, and flourished there especially among the English-speaking outposts. The organization reached a peak of participation and effectiveness in the late 19th century and in some areas forged tentative links with police forces and secret spy agencies.

One of the more bizarre rumors linked to the Light Society occurred in the early twentieth century. It involved the killing of a native from a remote part of South America said to have been invisible. (See Tribes of South America; The Invisible Tribe)

Colonel Jeremy Hornett described the event in a letter written just days before he died of gunshot wounds, said to have been self-inflicted.

'I tell you he was of flesh and blood and yet no body could be seen. I fired three volleys into mid-air, shooting at nothing but the strangled cries of a savage, and then there came the howling and moaning of a wounded man. And yet there remained not a single shred of evidence to suggest there was a man three yards from where I stood, though clearly to my mind he was there.

'In that moment I felt an unspeakable terror. As I stood, gripped in a cold fear such that I had never known before — there suddenly appeared from the ground the mortal image of a naked black man, his body streaked with blood. It was as if the very act of dying was in some macabre way bringing him

Tribe, The Invisible A remote tribe supposedly discovered by Elizabeth Graham (see File no. 6754.2.1 Graham, Elizabeth – adventurer). Field notes written by Graham in Portuguese were discovered by a Boston State Museum team in the Fundação Biblioteca Nacional in Brazil in 1993 detailing information about a tribe of people dwelling in a remote part of South America, supposedly with the ability to make themselves invisible. No direct evidence of the tribe has ever been established. Her notes, stolen from the Boston State Museum only a few months after they were lodged there, showed that settlers encroaching into the headwaters of the Amazon Basin were reporting the presence of creatures who communicated using high-pitched screams and shouts ('very human in nature'). However during the two days Graham spent listening (according to her notes) to these calls, she saw no other humans apart from herself and her local guides. Primate experts from the Boston State Museum propose that the noises were probably made by troops of monkeys and refuted claims that such a tribe exists. Elizabeth Graham vanished in the same area sometime during the 1990s. Little is known of the circumstances of her disappearance. (See also File no. 988776.43 *Tribes of the Amazon Basin*)

— or at least his body — to life. I raised my gun again and aimed it at the prostrate fellow, but I need not have concerned myself for but a moment later he breathed his last.

'A wild savage he was, but on my mother's grave I swear that for a moment, that native was not there and that I have this day confronted an invisible man. Or else I am going mad.'

The Light movement, with its interest in invisibility and secrecy, is known to have continued its search for the lost tribe but no record has ever surfaced detailing their success or otherwise.

Light membership reached its peak at around this time. But then the society suffered its first major set back. Carlos 'The Viper' Lento infiltrated a Light chapter in northern Italy. The knowledge he brought back to the criminal brotherhood led to the killing of over 400 Light members at a secret convention in Paris in 1907. Many other Light members were found brutally murdered in the months after the convention. The movement then seems to have gone to ground during the First World War, from which it recovered briefly before gradually dying out during the years between the World Wars.

Rumors circulated in the 1980s that the Light was re-forming but no conclusive evidence surfaced to substantiate these claims. A report of a secret gathering of Light members, referred to in one document as the Light Crusaders, with a particular interest in exploring the possibilities of secret identities using masks, circulated on the Internet for a few months in 2004. There were concerns about its more sinister frames of reference, though no evidence of such a group has ever been produced. A supposed link between the Light Crusaders and Masked Enterprises has been strongly denied by the manufacturing company. (See File no. #54327* *Raymond Brampton; Masked Enterprises; Masks — A Concise History*)

MASKED ENTERPRISES Established in 1893 by Sir Walter Brampton, Masked Enterprises began in East London, Great Britain as a manufacturer of synthetic masks for burns patients. The company soon broadened its range to include masks for theater, high society parties and even disguise.

During the First World War, Sir Walter and his son John began experimenting with seamless masks manufactured from material that emulated the look and feel of real skin. The masks could not only hide the identity of the wearer but also create a copy of an existing feature.

During the early 1960s, the company expanded world-wide, setting up scientific and research laboratories in South Africa, Australia and France and becoming one of the first true multinationals, owing its allegiance to no single state. An investigation by the Federal Police in Australia in 2003 failed to find any evidence to support allegations that bodies were being stolen from a morgue in Stanhope for the purpose of creating new identities. It was alleged that faces were being copied using an advanced laser and digital imaging technology.

Under the directorship of Sir Raymond Brampton, the company has continued to grow and in the last financial year recorded profits in excess of US$ 2.3 billion. Masked Enterprises holds major contracts for theater masks, surgical masks, burn treatments and the supply of specialized equipment for transplants with most Western governments and many non-governmental organizations throughout the developing world. The company was recently highly commended as a global business enterprise for the funds and resources it was contributing to protect the rainforests and indigenous tribes of the Amazon Basin in South America. 67

1

Amanda's Letter
— Part One

13 SEPTEMBER, 10.23 P.M.

The students at Bridgewater College had long since left the classrooms and corridors for the day and the building lay cold and empty. Even the noise and bustle of the boarding house had settled. The lights were out in the quarters of the younger children and weary students throughout the college were drifting off to sleep. One, though, was very much awake.

Lewis Watt slowly withdrew the neatly folded sheets of paper, his hands trembling. He stared again at his name carefully written on the front of the envelope. The letter had fallen out of a pigeonhole on Jonathan's desk while he'd been rummaging through its drawers looking for an eraser. Lewis quickly shuffled through to the last of the thin, faded sheets of paper and glanced at the name of its author.

He gasped. With a feeling of dread — and some excitement — he adjusted the small book light in his hand and started reading...

Only you, Lewis, could possibly believe the story I'm about to tell. And it's for you that I finally write it — before I disappear from this world completely. Of course you are closely woven into this world I am about to tell you about — I was pregnant with you as I stepped off the riverboat into the village of Novo Téfe on that fateful day.

Three days earlier we had flown into Sao Paulo on the east coast of Brazil. Our plan was to join a semi-official multidisciplinary expedition that was heading into a remote part of South America where the borders of Brazil, Colombia and Venezuela meet. From Sao Paulo we'd flown to Manaus and then taken a light plane to Boa Vista where several long riverboats and local guides took us north-west up the Uraricoera tributary and into the Sierra Pacaraima mountains.

A month or so earlier, when Fraser had returned from one of his increasingly frequent trips to Boston, he was desperate for us to join Professor Asher's expedition. Fraser, as you know, was a freelance journalist, publishing with some of the best magazines in New York and London. His essays were syndicated world-wide. He had combined degrees in history, science and journalism with a passion for research. He loved nothing better than to uncover a hidden document that would lead to a front-page story.

I'm not sure why, but for some reason I hesitated to join the expedition. Maybe I had a premonition. It was so out of character for Fraser to travel abroad. He really much preferred the libraries and coffee shops of the big cities, to roughing it in an uncharted wilderness.

The expedition was associated with one of the universities in Boston. Its primary objective was to search for new species of birds and plants. The area was particularly rich in orchids. That was Asher's main interest. Asher had also mentioned to Fraser that there was an outside chance of coming across a tribe of natives who'd never been seen by white people.

The expedition included a strange mix of people and, even though the group broke up after only three days, I remember them all so well. There was a couple from Germany and a group of three from New Zealand. We also had a local guide and of course Jonathan. I can remember being quite surprised by the German couple. They were so youthful and high-spirited, yet both were scientists of high renown.

We hiked nonstop for the first day, barely pausing long enough to enjoy the extraordinary surroundings. But as the terrain became steeper and wetter, our pace slowed so that we could better admire the plants and animal life of the forest. I won't bore you with the details, though I should mention Jonathan.

Of course, you know Jonathan like a father now. We owe him so much. What struck me when I met him was that he was so polite and cultured in that very English sort of a way. He kept to himself, with *his writings and his books. He was excited about the tribe, but in a completely different way to Fraser. His knowledge of the tribes and the fauna and flora of the area was astonishing. He had been to the area with Asher before and they seemed to know each other well, but there was some animosity between them. He wasn't part of the university but described himself as a simple school teacher.*

I have spoken to you many times about your father. He was a wonderful man; full of life and vigor. He was impulsive, daring, confident and fully assured of himself and the decisions he made. He had never liked being told what to do, but I thought that Fraser might be a little more conservative in a strange country. On the contrary. In fact, he was argumentative, fretful and insistent on doing things his way.

If only Fraser had listened to Jonathan.

Brilliant though he was, Fraser wasn't a tolerant man, especially with those he perceived to be not his intellectual equal. But this was a location where I thought Fraser might be a little more conservative — a little more willing to take on the advice of others. Others who, in this instance at least, knew more about the world we had entered than your father did. But no, that wasn't to be the case. But then, I didn't listen to Jonathan either, so who am I to accuse?

From the trip's outset, there was something about Fraser that worried me. In his pack was a strange collection of books that he let no one near. They were old, weathered books. I thought they might have been about witchcraft or voodoo. He caught me looking through one once and got very angry. I never looked again. He was possessive, uncommunicative and, for most of the time, distracted.

As I said, the first day and night were uneventful. But on the second day we saw an extraordinary range of wildlife. The colors of the birds were the richest and purest colors I'd ever seen. Toucans, macaws, kingfishers – we saw so many. Jonathan was able to identify the animals and birds by their strange cries. I won't ever forget the eerie honk of the scarlet macaw. And, of course, the long-tailed spider monkeys chattering away in the treetops, darting about the roof of the rainforest, were a constant distraction and I'm sure stopped us seeing many more birds.

Jonathan had his own map. I suspect that it was because of that map that we took some strange turnings that day, taking us away from the original track. At times there were no paths at all. Our surroundings grew quieter as we went deeper and deeper into the rainforest.

Later that afternoon our guide became nervous when we stumbled across an old burial site. Jonathan was excited, and so, I recall, was Fraser. It was quite frightening. I remember the strange shape of the ground and the odd-looking stone pillars arranged about the place. In the middle was a shallow grave. I got close enough to see the rotting flesh and exposed bones of a small body, lying on its side in the earth. I remember noticing the arm bones covering its skull. Was the poor child fending off blows? Protecting his head? A young Wandering Spider slowly crawled out of the child's rib cage.

'O tribe invisível,' our guide whispered in Portuguese, shaking.

Jonathan was suddenly very agitated, telling everyone to move back. Of course, Fraser did the opposite — striding into the clearing and heading straight for the grave.

'Fraser!' Jonathan called, anxiously.

But Fraser waved his arm dismissively and walked up to a wooden box sitting on top of one of the stone pillars. It was a casket, the size of a shoebox, and he strode to it without hesitation. He held it in his hands, then opened it dramatically; as if leading some religious ceremony.

I will never forget the look of anger and disappointment on his face.

Fraser stormed back to the group and refused to speak to anyone.

I wasn't close enough to discern what was actually in the box and neither Fraser nor Jonathan would say. Perhaps there was nothing. Perhaps that was why he was so disappointed. But what on earth had he been expecting? I was too afraid to ask.

What we didn't know during that strange series of events was that we were being watched. Maybe if Fraser hadn't opened the box — maybe then we would have been left alone and Fraser would still be alive today.

Maybe.

Returning to our camp, we set about preparing a fire and some food for dinner, enjoying the distraction. No one spoke of the clearing.

After dinner Jonathan explained his thoughts on the mystical burial ground to us. 'From what I can gather, this tribe lives and dies in shadow. They avoid the sun. They live and hunt at night. The height of the trees and the thickness of the canopy mean that no light ever penetrates the grave itself.'

'Why not just bury the body in the ground?' Freda, the young scientist from Germany asked.

'No one's sure,' Jonathan replied. 'There is so little known about the tribe.'

'This isn't the lost tribe we are looking for, is it?' I asked, looking from Jonathan to the guide.

No one answered me.

We leaned in closer to the fire. Jonathan was like a school boy — not the teacher we knew. Hunched over, arms clasped around his knees, his eyes darted from one to the other of us, shining and alive in the reflection of the fire light.

'We shouldn't have entered the clearing,' I said, looking at Fraser.

'What?' Fraser was angry. 'I took nothing.'

'Nothing?' Jonathan asked, eying him suspiciously.

'No!' snapped Fraser.

'Fraser?' I gasped, exasperated.

He looked me in the eye. I held his gaze, but his face

remained resolute. I knew Fraser. He could never lie without giving himself away. What I saw in his face was a lie.

That was the last time he spoke to me.

We had set up camp a few miles away from the burial ground.

'We should keep watch,' Fraser suggested.

Tamil, our guide, started to speak but was quickly interrupted by Jonathan. At the time it meant nothing. But of course I realize now why Jonathan had interrupted before Asher could comment. What was the point in keeping watch? Watching out for something you couldn't even see.

'That's a good idea,' Jonathan nodded, glaring at Tamil.

I wasn't awake when they arrived. Fraser was on watch. But suddenly I was alert, sitting upright in the tent. My senses were stretched to breaking point, listening for the slightest new sound against the constant background noise of the nocturnal crickets. Had I been dreaming or was that a muffled cry?

I peered out of the tent. I couldn't believe what I was seeing. Fraser was being dragged across *the clearing by some invisible force. I yelled, rushing outside. Suddenly Fraser flopped to the ground, as if he'd been dropped. There was a high-pitched whistling sound, almost like a scream. I turned as something, or someone came crashing through the undergrowth to my right.*

Fraser was struggling to his feet. By now, both Asher and Jonathan had arrived, as well as two of the men. I rushed over to Fraser who looked terrified. Just as he reached out to me, I heard the wail again. It was terrifying. Then Fraser's head jerked sideways like he'd been hit a terrible blow. He looked at me dazed, then collapsed to the ground. I remember his shocked expression and the dirt and dust that clung to his open mouth.

Is this too harsh for you to hear?

I am so sorry, Lewis, but I am recalling everything I can remember and writing it down here for you as Jonathan suggested. I want you to know and to understand everything.

One of our group fired a shot. Suddenly the wailing and high-pitched screaming was coming from all around us.

'Get into your tents!' Jonathan shouted.

'What about Fraser?' I screamed, trying to be heard above the awful shrieking.

'No!' Jonathan yelled, hauling me away from Fraser. 'Tamil, put the gun away!' Jonathan dragged me back towards the tent.

Tamil stood by his tent, gun raised, his whole body shaking. Suddenly Fraser was moving again. He looked like a puppet. It was as if someone was hiding in the trees way above us, pulling on strings attached to different parts of his body.

He was lying in the air. In mid-air. On his own. The gun fired again, and Fraser's left leg dropped suddenly, though he was still moving swiftly across the clearing and into the jungle to our left.

'Fraser!' I cried, trying to break free from Jonathan's grasp. But he held me firmly. 'For God's sake, let go of me. We can't just stand here!'

Suddenly the rainforest was silent again.

'They will kill us all. We cannot interfere.'

We argued back and forth until daybreak. Jonathan explained all he knew about the tribe and their extraordinary ability to become invisible.

Of course they are secret. Of course they are unknown. Unless you're an expert like Jonathan.

Asher had radioed through to his organizer and we were to be picked up later that morning. But I couldn't leave without knowing your father's fate, Lewis. I handed Fraser's gear to Asher to keep our packs light. By early morning I had convinced Jonathan that he had no control over my life — that I could never live with myself if I did not make some attempt to discover the fate of Fraser. Though his behavior had changed so much, I knew I wouldn't be able to live with myself if I didn't make some sort of effort to find him.

Or his body.

'Then I must go with you.'

The two of us set off before the sun had risen, following a trail of blood and branches broken by the natives marking their track. Asher had promised to engage the services of a private helicopter and return to the nearest landing area the next day. Jonathan fixed on a location. We had twenty-four hours to learn what we could.

We would need just one.

The rainforest was strangely quiet and heavy with humidity. After half an hour of walking, our clothes were drenched with sweat. I was about to *speak, but Jonathan held up a hand. He had heard or sensed something.*

'They are here,' he whispered, bending down on one knee.

'What now?' I breathed, crouching next to him.

Then suddenly, literally inches from my ear, came the horrible screaming sound of last night. I jumped in the air, never more frightened in my life.

'Don't struggle! Don't fight!' I remember Jonathan calling.

Hands were wrapping themselves around me, lifting me off the ground. Strong vice-like grips locked my ankles together. But there was no one there! It was a horrible dream.

'Jonathan!' I called.

The squealing started up again. Branches slapped and beat at me as I was carried through the bush, bouncing and bobbing high above the ground.

'Jonathan!' I screamed again.

There was no reply. It took only a few minutes until I arrived at the burial site we'd discovered yesterday. Roughly I was lowered to the ground, then forced onto my knees.

I was staring into the open pit where the child's

*rotting flesh and bones had been. But they were gone.
And in their place was Fraser. I called his name once,
but he didn't respond. His eyes stared straight through
me. He was dead.*

I must have fainted.

Lewis's head snapped up as a door slammed
shut. In the distance thunder rumbled. A storm
was approaching the town of Bridgewater.
A few of the students in the dormitory stirred
in their sleep, but no one woke. Lewis, normally
fearful of loud storms, hadn't even been aware
of it until the door had banged closed.

For a moment he lay trembling in bed,
recalling an early memory as a young child
when he'd been caught in a vicious storm.
The thunder and lightning and driving rain
were frightening. The fact that no one had
responded to his desperate and gut-wrenching
cries for help was worse. It had left in him
a lasting knot of doubt that surfaced whenever
a storm broke.

2

School Council Changes

Lewis tidied his notes and quickly made his way back to his seat, the applause still sounding in his ears. He'd just presented a talk on an item 'dear, special or significant' — another interesting topic from his English teacher, Mrs Jackson.

Lewis had only remembered that morning in the boarding house that the talk was due. He'd quickly snatched the tracking device from his desk on his way to class. He'd spoken without looking at his notes, but had everyone's attention — especially when he'd asked Abby to help demonstrate how it worked. He'd attached the device to Abby and asked her to leave the classroom and walk down to the library. His three-minute talk had turned into a thirty minute question-and-answer session. Even Mrs. Jackson had a turn at tracking.

'Thanks for your help, Ab,' said Lewis, back in his seat.

'No worries,' Abby whispered. She stood up to give her own presentation. 'That's a really hard act to follow.'

Lewis shrugged and smiled. 'I can't help it if I'm brilliant,' he said.

Out the front, Abby opened a large photo album and began her talk.

Lewis popped the tracker back into his pocket. The device had been a gift from Jonathan, his guardian and senior-school history teacher. Lewis had never met his real father. Jonathan was older than Lewis expected his real father to have been. And it was true that he wasn't into sport the way some fathers were. But he was Jonathan — always patient, generous and kind to Lewis.

Jonathan turned his attention to Abby and her photo album, enjoying her passionate presentation. The bell rang as she turned another page.

'It's blank,' someone called out.

'Exactly. They're for the photos that are yet to be taken. Sometimes it's just as interesting wondering what will go on these pages as looking at what's already there.' She closed the album and headed back to her seat.

'Questions and comments at the start of the next lesson,' Mrs. Jackson called out.

'Good one,' said Lewis.

'Not as good as yours,' said Abby.

Like Lewis, Abby Fleet was a long-term boarder at Bridgewater College. She was always talking, interested in everything going on around her. She asked questions Lewis never even thought to ask. And she liked Lewis, which was an absolute mystery to him.

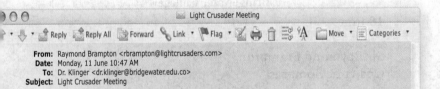
From: Raymond Brampton <rbrampton@lightcrusaders.com>
Date: Monday, 11 June 10:47 AM
To: Dr. Klinger <dr.klinger@bridgewater.edu.co>
Subject: Light Crusader Meeting

Dear Dr. Klinger,

I am delighted to inform you that we have chosen your school to become a meeting place for the Light Crusaders. Recently we have discovered certain items reside in your school that warrant further attention. There is also a teacher on the staff who I think may be able to assist us with our enquiries.

As a valued member of the Light community, you will appreciate that it is necessary for us, from a security point of view, to relocate our meeting places from time to time. This ensures we do not leave ourselves open to outsiders who might compromise our objectives.

It will be necessary to make some adjustments to the personnel on your school council to secure the school as a Light meeting place, though I am aware that some of your members are due to leave anyway.

Masked Enterprises would be delighted to support the school financially by sponsoring a conservation project in the Amazon jungles of South America. It is our aim that the intent will appear to be that of raising greater awareness of the threat to the Amazon rainforest by loggers and landowners. I know you are aware of the work my company does already in this area, so this will be a perfect cover for the development of the Light Crusaders' interest in the tribes of the Amazon Basin.

I look forward to our first meeting at Bridgewater College and trust that you will ensure a smooth transition to accommodate this new arrangement.

Raymond Brampton

29

Bridgewater College

18 June

Sir Raymond Brampton
Chalet de Sombras

Sir Raymond,

Thank you for your email, but I would prefer that you did not use this facility in future to contact me. My email is open to scrutiny by the Education Department at their whim and your emails could place me in an untenable position.

Bridgewater College would be delighted to be involved in projects that might raise awareness of diminishing rainforests and the effect on local flora and fauna and of course the indigenous peoples living in the Amazon Basin. However, there will be a number of formalities to be addressed before I can give the venture my full approval.

Making the changes necessary to allow for future meetings of the Light Crusaders to take place here at school — and in particular the changes you mention to the personnel of the school council — will take time.

Perhaps we can organize matters so that the Crusader meetings can begin at the start of next year, giving us both the necessary time to carefully and gently accommodate the changes you suggest. I look forward to your response.

Yours faithfully,

Dr. Deirdre Klinger
Principal

21 JUNE, 9.11 A.M.
DR. KLINGER'S RESIDENCE —
BRIDGEWATER

'Hello, is that Dr. Klinger?'

'It is. Who's speaking, please?'

'You don't recognise my voice, Dr. Klinger? I am surprised.'

Dr. Klinger paused. 'Sir Raymond?' she said, standing up suddenly. She had only spoken to the leader of the Light Crusaders once before.

'I am surprised and a little disappointed, Dr. Klinger. You appear to have lost vision of the Light,' the deep voice continued. 'I found your response to my request somewhat lacking in commitment.'

'Oh, I don't think so, Sir Raymond. It's just that these things take time, as I'm sure you understand.'

'I understand many things, Dr. Klinger. But time is not something that should ever get in the way of progress. It doesn't stand still and neither do I.'

'Well, of course ... I shall certainly speak to my council at the earliest opportunity.

But a school council is not simply a group of people...'

'I am aware of the role and function of a school council, Dr. Klinger. I look forward to meeting you in person. Perhaps you would care to pay me a visit at the Chalet de Sombras some time soon? I will arrange a date and let you know.'

The phone clicked dead. Dr. Klinger tried to remain calm, but the iciness in the leader's voice left her with a feeling of dread. What had caused this sudden interest in her school? Why would Raymond Brampton want to conduct Light Crusader meetings at Bridgewater College?

She glanced out her kitchen window. Jack, her gardener of seven years, was pruning a large rose bush. She breathed slowly, listening to the gentle click, click of his secateurs as he went about his work.

The rays of the morning sun warmed her as she stepped outside. She would talk to Morris Tate, a school councilor, on Monday. There was no need to bother him now. She was confident she could delay Raymond long enough so that he would soon change his mind about using the school as a venue for Crusader meetings. She had always felt it wise to keep her school and its students separate from the work of the Light. All she needed was time.

Still carrying her cell phone, she stepped into the garden.

'Jack,' she called, walking over to the rose garden, 'I think perhaps a little more can come off that bush.' She was surprised to see him quickly tuck a cell phone back into his shirt pocket.

Slowly Jack stood up and turned towards her. His face remained calm as he took two steps towards the school principal, then suddenly drew back his arm. Dr. Klinger frowned in bewilderment as her gardener raised his arm quickly and pressed a trigger, just inches from her. A cloud of icy spray covered her face. Gasping from the bitter-tasting mist, Dr. Klinger reeled away, her hands clawing at her eyes. Catching her as she fell back, Jack carefully walked the few paces back into her house, kicking the door shut behind him.

As the principal lay motionless on the floor, Jack calmly peered through the curtains. There was no one about. He wrenched the phone from the woman's hand, hit the calls received menu and put it to his ear.

'It is done, Raymond,' he said, smiling.

He would wait for the cover of night to remove the body.

Bridgewater College

25 June

Dear Parents,

Many of you will have heard of the unfortunate and quite sudden illness that Dr. Klinger suffered late last week. While more tests are to be completed, I am pleased to inform you that she is recovering well. Although not due back at school for some time yet, she is expected to make a steady but full recovery. She is grateful for the many warm wishes and sends her regards to everyone at Bridgewater College.

Dr. Klinger is recuperating in a health resort in the country and asks you to respect her request for privacy until she has recovered fully.

I trust that you will respect her wishes by not trying to get in touch with her.

Yours sincerely,
Lionel Thompson
(Acting Principal)

3

Chalet de Sombras

17 JULY, 4.35 P.M.

Special agent Tamsin Jennings surveyed the building carefully as she walked up the driveway. She had committed to memory both the manor's surroundings and all the rooms inside from the satellite images and diagrams she'd studied. It was a job she was competent at, but it was always exciting to finally be 'hot'; 'alive and in the zone' as she and her colleagues referred to it.

For eight months she had been leading

a covert operation studying the movements of Masked Enterprises, and in particular the Chalet de Sombras — the mansion owned by the entrepreneur Raymond Brampton. The heat-sensed images from the Secret Service's spy satellites had failed to pick up anything peculiar. It was up to Tamsin and her team of highly-trained RODA (Return or Die Alone) team agents to probe further into the working of the organization.

She rang a brass bell and turned to watch a group of women working in a field to the right of the building. None of them paid her the slightest attention.

'Welcome,' a woman dressed in a grey suit said, smiling and stepping aside for Tamsin to enter. 'You must be the journalist from the *New York Times*. My name is Zoe Westcott.' She extended her hand.

'Connie Rogers,' Tamsin smiled, presenting her with a journalist's pass.

They shook hands.

'May I take your pass?' the woman said smoothly. 'We must be careful about security.'

'Oh, why is that?' said Tamsin as she removed the pass from her neck and handed it to Zoe.

'The people who live here have left behind lives they do not wish to revisit. I hope you understand this. As my letter explained, we'd prefer it if you didn't interact in any way with the patients here.'

'I'm happy to follow your requirements,' said Tamsin. 'And I'm looking forward to bringing the amazing story of Chalet de Sombras to the whole world.'

Zoe nodded briskly. 'Many requests have been made for access to the Chalet de Sombras story. Your publication is the only one Mr. Brampton has admitted. He is anxious to dispel some negative reports that have emerged recently in the media.'

'I'm looking forward to my stay here immensely,' said Tamsin.

'As we are delighted to have you here.' Zoe smiled, then marched across the entrance hall.

'I doubt that,' Tamsin thought following the woman up a wide circular staircase.

Local man lucky to be alive

BRIDGEWATER: A 45-year-old man is in a critical condition at the Bridgewater Base Memorial Hospital after crashing his car into a tree on Talisman Road last night. The driver, Peter Robinson, is a prominent local businessman recently appointed to the school council at Bridgewater College. Mr Robinson sustained multiple-fractures, internal bleeding and burns to over 40 per cent of his body, but is expected to make a full recovery. Mr Robinson is well-known for his strong views on a variety of civil issues and his forthright opinions have alienated him from some sections of the community. A spokesperson for the Robinson family has stated that his vehicle has been impounded for analysis. 'We will leave no stone unturned,' his son Damien said late last night. 'My father is an excellent driver and the road conditions were fine. He doesn't drink and has never been given a speeding ticket. We view the whole situation as highly suspicious.' The police have refused to speculate.

BRIDGEWATER COLLEGE

The council would like to pass on their condolences to the Ramsay family after the sudden death of James Ramsay, last Sunday. He will be remembered for his dedication and commitment to the school over a number of years. From his involvement in various sporting teams, his leadership of the Bridgewater Carnival and his work for many years as a school councilor, James has made a lasting contribution to our school and will be sadly missed by all who had the good fortune to have crossed his path during his time at our school.

Staff News

We congratulate Fiona Langdon on her appointment to the position of Corporate Affairs Manager for Complete Airways. Fiona has been working in one of our regional offices for the past nine years. She will be sorely missed by many sections of the community in the city of Bridgewater where she contributed to a variety of areas including the Youth Centre, SSM (Support for Single Moms), Bridgewater Conservation Group and the local dramatic society, Bridgewater Theater. She was also a hard-working member of the Bridgewater College school council for many years. Best wishes Fiona as you take on a new and exciting challenge in your career.

Bridgewater College

19 July

Dear Margaret,

It is with deep regret that I must inform you of a decision made in light of recent events involving your daughter, Miranda. It is with great sadness, not least because of our own friendship and your wonderful involvement on the school council, that I inform you of my decision to discontinue Miranda's enrolment here at the College. She is to be expelled from the school effective from this Friday, 21 July.

Miranda has recently been involved in a range of incidents detrimental to the good reputation of this school. Both her teachers and I feel that the negative influence she is having on other students is untenable. Her most recent 'prank' was an act of gross misconduct that left me with no choice. My concern is for the safety of the students here.

Of course, I will have to accept your resignation from the school council in light of these most unfortunate events. May I take this opportunity to thank you for your work on council.

I know Miranda has many fine qualities that may yet be nurtured in a different kind of school environment. I do wish you and Miranda strength for this difficult time ahead.

Yours sincerely,

Lionel Thompson
(Acting Principal)

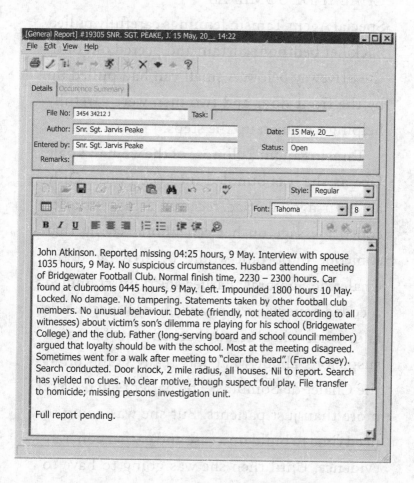

[General Report] #19305 SNR. SGT. PEAKE, J. 15 May, 20__ 14:22

File   Edit   View   Help

Details | Occurence Summary

File No: 3454 34212 J   Task:
Author: Snr. Sgt. Jarvis Peake   Date: 15 May, 20__
Entered by: Snr. Sgt. Jarvis Peake   Status: Open
Remarks:

Style: Regular
Font: Tahoma   8

B *I* <u>U</u>

John Atkinson. Reported missing 04:25 hours, 9 May. Interview with spouse 1035 hours, 9 May. No suspicious circumstances. Husband attending meeting of Bridgewater Football Club. Normal finish time, 2230 – 2300 hours. Car found at clubrooms 0445 hours, 9 May. Left. Impounded 1800 hours 10 May. Locked. No damage. No tampering. Statements taken by other football club members. No unusual behaviour. Debate (friendly, not heated according to all witnesses) about victim's son's dilemma re playing for his school (Bridgewater College) and the club. Father (long-serving board and school council member) argued that loyalty should be with the school. Most at the meeting disagreed. Sometimes went for a walk after meeting to "clear the head". (Frank Casey). Search conducted. Door knock, 2 mile radius, all houses. Nil to report. Search has yielded no clues. No clear motive, though suspect foul play. File transfer to homicide; missing persons investigation unit.

Full report pending.

18 JULY, 3.55 A.M.

CHALET DE SOMBRAS

Special Agent Tamsin Jennings carefully pulled back her bedroom curtain and peered out onto the driveway below. A small van had pulled up by the front door and two men were carefully helping a woman up the steps.

Tamsin caught a glimpse of the woman's pale face as she was bundled into the house. Only an hour ago she had received a high-priority coded message on her cell phone saying that someone important would be arriving at the Chalet de Sombras. Earlier she'd unscrambled a coded report on a phantom newspaper site and what she'd read backed up her own suspicions about what was really going on at the Chalet de Sombras. The patients here were more than just patients. But she was going to need time to build up a case and gather concrete evidence. Until then she was going to have to remain calm and, more importantly, hidden.

Of course she had read about the illness the school principal had suffered. Dr. Klinger was currently under surveillance as a possible member of The Light Crusaders. She'd seen Dr. Klinger's picture in her reports. Why was it then that Dr. Klinger had arrived here, at such a strange hour?

Someone tapped gently on her door. Tamsin raced to the bed and dived under the blanket as a key gently turned in the lock.

'Miss Rogers?' a female voice called, softly.

Tamsin feigned sleep, keeping her breathing slow and even as she sensed Zoe move closer to the bed. Suddenly Tamsin shot bolt upright in bed and swung around, her arms poised.

'Oh,' Tamsin gasped, pretending to be shocked and dropping her arms quickly. 'What is it? Is something wrong?'

'You have to leave,' Zoe Westcott said flatly. 'I was coming to wake you up.'

'Why? It's the middle of the night.'

'I'm terribly sorry, but a situation has arisen that threatens to compromise the safety of our patients. We are preparing an evacuation. I will wait for you outside.'

'What situation?' Tamsin called, but Zoe appeared to not have heard her.

Zoe left the room abruptly as her cell phone started to ring.

Tamsin dressed and packed quickly, checking carefully that she'd left nothing behind. This had to have something to do with the arrival of the principal, she thought, glancing out the window again. The van was still parked outside. Perhaps she could use this to her advantage. She swung her overnight bag onto her shoulder and released the handle on her trolley bag so she could pull it behind her.

'We'll have to go the other way,' Zoe said to her as soon as Tamsin opened the door.

Tamsin peered past her shoulder and over the rail of the landing to a group of people gathered in the entrance hall below. It was quite a party for four in the morning. Tamsin looked again and frowned.

'Now, Miss Rogers.'

Tamsin felt a hand firmly clasp her arm.

'I left a pair of running shoes down by the door,' Tamsin said, breaking free from Zoe's grasp and moving towards the top of the stairs.

'Stop!' The tone in the woman's voice surprised Tamsin. Faces from below looked up. But she'd seen enough.

'Hey, it's okay. I'm sorry,' Tamsin said, shaking her head and following Zoe Westcott back past her bedroom.

For a split-second Tamsin had caught sight of the principal, Deirdre Klinger, smiling broadly and talking animatedly to a man standing next to her. The man was Raymond Brampton. She was wearing different clothes than those she was wearing on her arrival. Tamsin thought the woman seemed a little taller. Had she just seen first-hand exactly what was going on here? The transformation of one person into another using the special technology available at Masked Enterprises?

Tamsin smiled to herself. The woman laughing in the hall was not the school principal. It all fitted perfectly. She was a double, made to look like the principal.

Perhaps all the 'patients' here were doubles — people pretending to be other people. But for what purpose? Tamsin stopped suddenly.

Perhaps there was a way this sudden change of events could be made to work in her favour. She would have to act quickly.

Tamsin followed Zoe Westcott through the kitchen to the garage behind the house. Suddenly Tamsin sensed danger. Call it instinct, or years of training, but it suddenly became clear to her that she was never supposed to be leaving the Chalet de Sombras alive tonight. Perhaps it was their intention that she would never have been leaving the place alive.

Reaching into her pocket for her keys, Tamsin flicked the remote of her car on. The lights blinked once and the door locks snapped open.

'Well, Miss Rogers,' Zoe said coldly, breaking into Tamsin's thoughts. 'I'm so sorry we've had to cut your visit short like this. Just when it appeared you were gathering some useful information.'

Tamsin moved quickly towards her car.

'I don't know what—'

'There's no need to pretend, Miss Rogers. Or should I call you Tamsin Jennings...?'

Tamsin didn't wait for the woman to finish. Noticing Zoe's hand reach inside her jacket, Tamsin picked up her overnight bag and hurled it at the woman. Startled, Zoe lifted her arms as the bag hurtled towards her face. The impact sent her staggering back. Knowing it would only be seconds before someone arrived, Tamsin grabbed the woman firmly, driving a knee into her temple before she could get to her feet. It was critical that Zoe was removed from the area so Tamsin's escape remained a secret. Of course, Zoe would be missed back at Chalet de Sombras eventually...

Tamsin hauled the woman's limp frame into the back seat, jumped behind the wheel of the car and set off. She checked her rear-view mirror several times, then leant forward and flicked a switch to the left of the dashboard. She retrieved an ear-piece from the glove box.

'Casey, we have red alert. The mission has been compromised. Request immediate back up, but stay out of range till further instructions.' She flicked the switch of the microphone off and steered the car smoothly towards the gate at the end of the driveway. She had just turned onto another unsealed road when she noticed a beam of light in the distance behind her. Another car, perhaps the van, had left the property and was speeding towards her.

After stopping the car in the middle of the road, Tamsin jumped out and ran to a cover of trees beyond a ditch. She watched the van ease up and slow to a halt behind her car. A man hopped down from the driver's seat. Another person was waiting in the passenger seat.

'Come on, come on,' she whispered, urging the man closer to her vehicle.

'Zoe?' he called out, looking around.

Tamsin stared at the rear window of her car. She hoped Zoe would not choose that moment to wake up from the blow to her head, but there was no movement from the car.

Silently Tamsin left the darkness of the trees, moving parallel to the road and back towards the van.

'Zoe?' he shouted, louder. The man paused and turned at the sound of a faint cry.

Suddenly Tamsin was running flat out for the van. Too late, the man realized the situation as Tamsin jumped into the cabin.

'Don't,' she snapped, noticing the woman beside her reach for something under the seat. Ramming the gear stick into first gear and gunning the accelerator, Tamsin guided the van past her hastily parked car.

'Two suspects need cleansing as does my vehicle,' she said quickly into her ear-piece then glanced quickly at her rear-view mirror. 'They're in the driveway leading up to the Chalet de Sombras. How far away are you?' Tamsin steered the van out onto the main road. 'Good.'

The back-up team was closer than she thought.

'Dr. Klinger?' Tamsin said, turning to the woman seated beside her. 'I'm so glad I was able to rescue you.' And you don't know how to react, Tamsin thought.

'Who sent you?' the woman asked Tamsin.

'Raymond Brampton, of course,' Tamsin replied, keeping her eyes on the road ahead of her. The rest of her team would arrive within moments to clean up the mess she'd left behind. No one need realize that 'Dr. Klinger' was about to undergo yet another transformation. She just hoped that the real Dr. Klinger was safe. If everything went according to plan, there was no reason to suspect that there would be any problems at the Chalet de Sombras.

'But Raymond never told me about this? Where are we going?'

'Of course he didn't. Secrecy is of the utmost importance.'

The Dr. Klinger double leant back in her seat. She knew better than to question the decisions that Raymond Brampton made.

Principal Suffers Gardening Collapse

'I kept myself hidden while I recuperated. I didn't want to worry the students.'

BRIDGEWATER: The mystery surrounding the disappearance of Deidre Klinger has a happy conclusion. Speaking from her bed at the Chatham City Private Hospital, the principal of Bridgewater College has told of her remarkable brush with death. In a statement made to the media, the principal tells of a spell of dizziness which caused her to fall in her front garden. It was fortunate that a passer-by noticed her lying on the garden path. The identity of the person who discovered Doctor Klinger is unknown but it is believed that he received a request from the principal that nothing be said of the matter for fear of worrying her students. She has undergone a range of tests relating to her immune system. She is expected to make a full recovery and return to duties at Bridgewater College in three weeks.

19 AUGUST, 9.42 A.M.

'Welcome everyone to our first school council meeting for the term,' Dr. Klinger said, gazing intently from face to face around the large, polished antique table. She smiled thinly. 'A number of you are new to this role and I extend my warmest and most sincere thanks for responding so quickly to our call.'

There were smiles and knowing nods from the various members. The smell of freshly brewed coffee filled the air. The spacious room was lit by a number of lamps, glowing softly on small tables around the room.

One of the new council members glanced outside. Dark clouds were gathering. He watched a group of students huddled in close, hugging themselves and running on the spot, trying to keep warm as they listened to their teacher. Rain tapped at the glass. He turned back to the principal, easing his jacket off his shoulders and smiled. It was warm inside the Matthew Pescott Room, where the school council meeting was taking place.

'As you know, we have suffered a number of

losses in the membership of the council, for a variety of reasons. Please welcome our newly elected head of school council, Morris Tate.'

There was a polite smattering of applause.

Dr. Klinger continued. 'But I'm sure the group here today will do a more than adequate job in fulfilling the duties of a school council. Each of you has responsibility for a particular area and will report to each meeting on the business arising from your field. This is your cover. We must maintain the duties a council performs. Your roles are outlined in the folders in front of you. But, of course, there is another matter that I know each of you is extremely interested in that will take up most of our time.'

She paused, looking about as if the curtains, plants or other pieces of furniture might be somehow listening. But that was impossible. An associate of Raymond's had swept the room for bugs thoroughly just three days ago and had returned yesterday and spent two hours meticulously searching the room again. He'd found nothing.

Dr. Klinger pressed a button on a glass remote control. Small shades in each of the windows gently rotated to a half-closed position as the room slowly grew lighter. A series of eight spotlights embedded in the ceiling directly above the table slowly brightened.

'The Light,' she said. 'This is the signal that our discussions will move from school matters to matters of the Light.'

The council members smiled at her. There was a feeling of anticipation and excitement in the room, the principal thought, enjoying her role.

'Shall we begin?' she said, closing the gray folder and pressing another button on the remote. The lights dimmed again as a large white screen slowly descended from the ceiling at the far end of the room. 'We shall start with a message from Mr. Brampton.'

Dr. Klinger pressed a button on a recorder and sat back in her chair.

'Greetings all of you. The Crusaders of Light, together again, and with good reason. We are small in number and maintain our anonymity. And if we are successful in our quests then we shall continue to remain anonymous.

'We are on the brink of a monumental discovery and that discovery will take place here at the very school where you sit now. A secret of such far-reaching magnitude that the world may never be the same again.

'We must proceed with care but also with haste. The man who possesses this secret works at Bridgewater College. He is also the guardian of a student there — one Lewis Watt. The teacher's name is Jonathan Ramshaw. He is our connection to South America, to the Invisible Tribe and to the secret of the power of invisibility.

'Jonathan Ramshaw has been hiding his secret here at this school for nearly 25 years. But no more.

'In a room not far from you sits an old South American relic: a casket. It is my belief that the secret lies within that casket. I have read every available document and text that there is to read on the matter, though I fear many still elude me. I won't bore you with the details of the investigation. Suffice to say that those who need to know certain things will be informed at the appropriate time. We are at a critical point and no one is to act without my prior approval. I hope that is understood.

'We must be ruthless in our quest, my fellow Crusaders. If it means that sacrifices must be made along the way, then so be it. Remember, it is for the greater good. We must maintain and uphold that mantra at all times and keep it at the forefront of our minds.

'Thank you for your attendance tonight. From small things do great things flourish. We are the Light Crusaders and our mission of eradicating the darkness has begun.'

Dr. Klinger switched off the recorder and smiled at the expectant faces looking back at her. 'We shall begin by discussing the school's involvement with the conservation projects for the Amazon Basin in South America,' she said, opening a folder on the table in front of her. 'This work has suddenly taken on new meaning as I'm sure you will understand.'

In the corridor outside the Matthew Pescott Room, Martin Caldor, the school's recently appointed head cleaner, slowly made his way towards the tea room, limping slightly. He glanced through a small window onto the courtyard below. The rain had become heavier and a gloomy darkness had settled over the school. He switched a fluorescent tube on in the corridor and shuffled into the tea room, muttering to himself about the lack of light.

Amanda's Letter — Part Two

13 SEPTEMBER, 10.29 P.M.

Lewis rolled over onto his stomach and continued reading. Outside, rain spattered on the windows.

I woke to the sound of that awful wailing. It was raining — a hard, beating rain that crashed onto the roof of the small hut I was trapped in. And this is the strange thing — I knew I was in a hut; I could hear the rain beating down on its roof, yet I couldn't see it! It was the strangest and most bewildering thing. I sensed the walls around me, yet could not see them.

I shouted. 'Let me go! Help! Let me out of here!'

But no one came. For hours and hours I called to both Jonathan and Fraser, but there was never an answer. Had Jonathan been captured like me? Or had something worse happened? Never for a moment did I imagine that he might have escaped. How could he and then not return for me?

My imprisonment seemed to last for ever. They hadn't bothered to tie me down. There was no need. My prison seemed impenetrable. Now and again, but never at regular intervals, I was given foul water, grubs and shreds of uncooked meat. At first I only drank the water, but soon managed to eat and keep down the scraps of food they left beside me. Once I tried to escape to the space I imagined to be the doorway, only to be pushed down to the ground. I picked at the scattered food on the dirt floor and ate — no water that night. I did it for your sake, Lewis. Had I not been pregnant I think I would have given up — refused their meagre offerings. But I drank the foul-tasting water so you might one day live. And I ate their stinking meat and other sickly concoctions to give you strength. Hope is an extraordinary thing, Lewis. Lose hope and you lose the spirit to live. I never lost hope, though I came awfully close.

Day after day I endured their hateful screaming. At first I was scared, but I soon came to loathe and despise them. I could sense them moving about me, whispering in their strange language. I swore at them, abused them and called them every possible rude word I could think of. But I might as well have been telling them the color of my bedroom wall back home. They didn't understand a word.

Then one night, I guess it to be about a week later, I heard someone enter the shack. I gasped. Was this person one of the tribe? Although I couldn't see a body, the person was carrying a flaming torch and the flickering light illuminated a deathly pale mask that covered, what I guessed to be, an invisible face.

I was grabbed roughly by the arm and hauled outside. I could hear the murmurings of other tribe members coming from a clearing where a fire crackled. I could feel its warmth. I was taken to the clearing and forced to lie down on the ground. I could see only the one masked face but I could sense the presence of many people moving about, *whispering and chatting in high-pitched voices. Was this to be the end?*

'Fraser!' I shrieked, so loudly that for a moment all other noise stopped. The echo of my voice drifted through the dense rainforest then all was silent again.

*Suddenly strong hands were pinning down my arms and legs. I closed my eyes and mumbled a quiet prayer. A voice hissed strange noises close to my ear and I felt a sticky substance being **rubbed** on my arms and legs, and then my face. It **was** hot and **cold**; light and heavy. It was something, yet **nothing**.*

More strange words were spoken and then I felt a burning sensation, starting near my feet that quickly raced up through my body. I wriggled and squirmed, desperately fighting to break free from the strong arms that held me, but it was no use. I must have passed out. When I woke again, I was back in the hut.

Back in darkness.

But nothing seemed to have changed. I felt no different. The liquid on my skin and the burning sensation had left no apparent marks.

I spent every waking moment thinking about the tribe, trying to keep my mind occupied and alert.

Mentally I gathered everything I knew about the invisible tribe. Some members wore special masks to present a visible face to the world.

The night was their friend. Were they able to move from visibility to invisibility at will? How could they do this? Were they born invisible? How did they become invisible? Were they evil? Or just frightened of someone they'd not encountered before?

Days passed. Of course having you so close to me was a blessing and a curse. If only we could survive this horrific nightmare, I promised us both, then we would never, ever travel abroad again.

I had lost all sense of time but I think it must have been another four or five days before, finally, my dark world changed. I was finding it increasingly difficult to distinguish between dreams and reality so that when I first heard a frantic voice whispering close to my head, I turned away, covering my ears with my hands to ward off the hallucination. But the voice persisted.

'Amanda, it's me!'

I stiffened. Could it be?

'Jonathan?' I breathed, my voice the barest whisper. 'Is it really you?'

'We've not much time.'

A hand covered my mouth. He knew I'd scream the moment I turned.

'You're invisible,' I gasped, reaching out. 'But how?'

'Come on,' he said. 'I won't be for much longer. Look at my feet.'

I glanced down at the floor, swaying slightly, dizzy with light-headedness. The faintest image of a bare foot appeared then disappeared as I stared at the ground.

'Don't speak.'

I was falling, but Jonathan's invisible hand clasped me by the arm and I felt myself being dragged out of the hut. It was early morning, and the barest hint of sunlight filtered through the treetops to the rainforest floor. Dawn was breaking. The clearing was deserted.

We ran.

Jonathan was pulling me along a narrow path that wound its way steeply down towards a river.

On and on we ran, crashing through the dense rainforest. Finally, when I thought I could run no further, we stopped. I was over being frightened. Being dragged through the South American rainforest *by an invisible man felt as normal as anything else I'd done during the past ten days.*

I felt myself being lifted off my feet as the shrieks of the tribe echoed through the rainforest. I sensed Jonathan's fear and wondered briefly what they would do to us if we were caught.

On and on we ran, but I was slow and the cries of the warriors pursuing us were getting closer by the minute. Jonathan still held me firmly by the hand.

'I... I can't go on,' I breathed, more to myself.

I fell to the ground. My body, useless after days of inactivity, was spent. I was nearing exhaustion. From behind me suddenly, an arrow whistled past my head, spearing a tree just a few feet to my left. Another crashed through the branches above me. I felt Jonathan's grip relax and then let go. Had he been struck by an arrow?

With one last monumental effort I dragged myself to my feet and stumbled on. The sound of crashing branches told me that Jonathan was alive and only just ahead.

The cries of the tribesmen seemed only a few feet away.

'Jonathan?' I screamed.

It was like I'd cast a spell. All of a sudden their strange voices stopped. I pressed on, but only managed a few feet before losing my footing. Suddenly I was toppling over the edge of a ravine that had sprung up from nowhere, tumbling and rolling down through a mixture of palm fronds, mud, leaves and water, before crashing into a river.

Plunging into the water caused every bruise and wound on my body to pulsate with intense pain but I managed to keep my mouth closed as I went under, somehow catching a small gulp of air before sinking into the river's murky depths. Knowing that the warriors were probably watching from the top of the ravine, I started to wade under water — trying to put as much distance between me and the hunters.

The pains eased slightly, the water helping to revive my energy and spirit. Five more strokes, I said to myself, wading further out towards the middle of the water where the current was stronger.

Then something thick and slippery slithered past my leg. Spinning round I tried to peer into the brown, brackish water, at the same time thrusting a hand down to push away the thing that was pressing against me. But it wasn't a reed. It was an enormous snake — as thick as a man's leg and long and sleek. It had quickly wrapped itself around my thigh and was squeezing hard.

As I broke the surface, gasping for air, I felt something sharp graze my body, but a second later I was pulled back under by the snake.

Quickly spinning around I smashed my leg and the snake against the rock I'd just bumped. But if anything, its grip tightened. My left leg was going numb. Again I tried to push the snake against the rock. This time I must have found a sharper piece for its hold on me momentarily loosened.

There was a horrible thrashing as the snake jerked and writhed in the water. Again and again I cut the snake against the rock, trying to tear the creature off my leg, but after the initial victory, I sensed its hold on me beginning to tighten yet again.

Gasping for air before my head was dragged below, I reached down into the water trying to beat the horrible creature with my fists. But it was no use. It was now almost completely wrapped around my leg; a giant, throbbing mass of slippery flesh, crushing my limb.

A sickening wave of nausea and icy calm swamped

me as I was pulled deep down into the darkness of the river. I closed my eyes and relaxed, the will to fight vanishing suddenly. Nothing mattered any more. In that moment I gave up. My body went limp as I succumbed to my fate in this watery grave.

Then something sharp and needle-like brushed my face. I opened my eyes, even at this depth glimpsing the razor sharp teeth of a small fish. Then there was another. In a matter of seconds the water was alive with hundreds of these tiny fish.

I felt myself floating upwards, the weight on my leg suddenly lifted. Thrashing with my arms, I propelled myself to the surface, ignoring the sharp, stinging pains as hundreds of small fish began tearing at the flesh of my arms and legs.

My head finally clear of the water, I looked around desperately. The water was alive with thousands of tiny bubbles creating a whirlpool of blood, froth and frenzy. I screamed as the snake suddenly started jerking, wrenching and pulling as it tried desperately to keep its hold of my leg. But the flesh-eating fish were tearing it open. In a matter of seconds the crushing pressure on my leg eased.

Gasping with relief as my leg suddenly felt free and

light, I paddled towards the rock. Brushing away the small fish, I hauled myself onto the rock, smashing two of them against the hard surface as I scrambled up on top of it.

I looked back in horror at the turbulent water, realising how close I had come to being eaten alive. But it was the snake that was now being eaten by a swarm of tiny piranha fish. A stab of searing pain in my left hand caused me to almost overbalance and fall back into the feeding mayhem. Smashing my hand against the rock, I crushed the last of the fish, its little belly bursting. Its jaw slackened and I gently eased its razor-sharp teeth from my hand before flicking it back into the water.

My body was covered in their tiny pin-pricks, but thankfully it had been the snake that had their attention. Maybe they weren't used to the taste of human flesh. In no time, the feasting frenzy calmed as the piranha quickly devoured the snake.

Shivering, I looked back up into the trees at the top of the ravine. All appeared quiet.

Had the warriors assumed that I would drown? Or be eaten alive?

There were no more arrows, and when I next

heard their fearsome cries, ten minutes later, they were distant. Managing to crawl from the rock to an enormous fallen tree, I lay back, exhausted. The early morning sun beamed down, drying my sodden clothes.

It was the first time I'd felt its warmth for almost two weeks. Perhaps it was a sign that my nightmare was finally coming to an end. I closed my eyes. Thirty minutes, I promised myself, no more.

Lewis shivered despite the warmth of the room. Someone in the dormitory called out. Startled, Lewis suddenly looked up. He'd been so engrossed in his mother's letter that he'd forgotten where he actually was.

A window shutter was banging outside. Reluctantly he crawled out of bed and went over to shut it properly. Outside, the wind howled. A flash of lightning briefly lit the room followed by a loud crack of thunder. With his head down, Lewis jumped into bed, pulling the blanket up over his shoulders as he scrambled back into its warmth. He switched on his flashlight to read the letter.

5

In the Dead of Night

28 AUGUST, 3.36 A.M.

A gloved hand gently turned the door handle of the Bridgewater School Library. There was a soft click. Slowly pushing the glass door open, the man stepped into the library. He knew what he was looking for and he knew exactly where to locate it.

Striding silently but purposefully across the polished floor, he came to another door. He had no key for this door, but he had something equally useful.

Opening up a small black briefcase, he took out a thin, silver pen. Switching it on, the man adjusted the needle-thin beam of red light by slowly turning the laser intensity dial. The instrument hummed softly.

Donning a pair of dark, protective glasses, he guided the laser beam into a narrow gap, aiming the light at the heavy bolt that bridged the gap between the door and the door jamb. The beam intensified as the man gently squeezed the trigger, glowing a brighter orange as it sliced through the bolt like a hot knife through butter. For a moment, the bolt flashed a blinding white. Seconds later the thick bolt had been split in two, a thin wisp of acrid black smoke coiling upwards before disappearing into the air.

He switched the laser off and returned it to his briefcase. Pausing briefly, he listened for any sounds but the library was silent.

He entered the smaller room, walking quickly to a glass cabinet.

Once more he opened his briefcase, this time removing a tiny glass cutting machine. Its suction cups squeezed down with a soft sound as he placed it carefully on the glass, directly above the casket. It was the casket he had come to collect.

Its secret had remained unknown to all but the history teacher, but that was about to change. In a few moments the man would be holding the key to perhaps the most powerful secret that any human had held in mankind's history. A secret so immense it would change the course of history like nothing else before it.

He had been patient, making sure the new principal and changes to the school council were well and truly settled before commencing this second stage of the operation.

The man guided the glass cutter, watching it slice a neat rectangle slightly larger than the wooden casket that lay just ten inches below. The small vacuum attached to the cutter quietly sucked in the minuscule fragments of glass spraying into the air as the machine raced along the top of the glass.

Carefully the man lifted the glass section

out, still attached to the four suction cups that held it firmly. He closed his eyes briefly. His hands shaking slightly, he reached into the cabinet and took hold of the casket, lifting it gingerly out of its resting place.

It was surprisingly heavy. The man stared at it in wonder, perplexed that there appeared to be no locking mechanism.

Then something caught his eye. A red, flashing light coming from the main section of the library. The man quickly released the glass from the suction cups, returned the glass cutter to his briefcase and snapped it locked. He had insisted that the theft be made to actually look like a legitimate break-in. He'd even told the principal to leave the alarm on. By his calculations, he had several minutes left before the alarm was activated.

With the casket tucked securely under his right arm, he walked quickly back towards the door. A noise suddenly blared out above him — he had miscalculated.

Looking up, he realized the noise was coming from a smoke detector, directly above the door to the Reference Library — the door he'd lasered through just a moment ago. Though he could see no smoke, the smell of burnt metal still lingered.

Perhaps the trail of smoke had traveled closer to the ceiling than he thought. Calmly, but swiftly, the man walked back to the main door and slipped out into the darkness of the night.

Three minutes later he was driving swiftly along the main highway out of Bridgewater. He pressed a button to activate the electronic window. In the distance he heard a siren wailing.

He traveled just under the speed limit for fifteen minutes before pulling into a wayside stop twenty miles south of Bridgewater. The man parked the car well away from the road, doused the lights and for a moment sat still, enjoying the silence.

It was 2.45 in the morning. The man paused, waiting for a car to sweep by, then got out and approached the trunk of his car. Shining the beam of the flashlight on the casket, the man frowned. He wondered again where the lock was.

Hesitantly he reached out and slowly eased the lid open, surprised that something so valuable should be so easy to penetrate. Surely there was more to it than that? A trap? He sensed the lights of another car approaching and switched off the flashlight. Tucked away close to a copse of trees, the man was confident that he couldn't be seen. He just didn't need anyone to decide that this wayside curb would be a good place to stop for a rest. The car swept over the rise. The man watched its red rear lights disappear into the distance before turning his attention back to the casket.

He was delaying. He smiled to himself, surprised at his sudden nervousness. He was perhaps on the brink of the most profound moment of his life. There would be time later for others to come to know about his discovery. Now was his moment. He'd trust no one else with this mission.

Gently taking the lid of the casket in his hands, he pushed firmly upwards. There was a moment of resistance before the lid came away. With trembling hands, the man shone his flashlight inside the wooden chest.

His heart leapt at the sight of an old parchment, neatly folded, leaning against one side of the box. With trembling hands he carefully withdrew the paper and unfolded it. It was blank. There was nothing but mould and dirt stains. Turning it over he saw that the other side was exactly the same.

Stifling a cry of disappointment the man angled the flashlight into the corners. Nothing. Nothing but empty space. Furious, he tossed the blank piece of paper back into the chest and slammed the lid shut. He hurled the flashlight into the trunk, threw the trunk down and marched around to the driver-side door.

His trip back to Bridgewater took only ten minutes.

29 AUGUST, 8.22 A.M.
Dr. Klinger tapped a spoon against the side of a glass and the noise in the staff room quickly subsided.

'Some of you may be aware that the school was broken into last night,' she said, looking carefully around the room at the faces of her staff. Her eyes rested on Jonathan Ramshaw, the Head of History. 'Thankfully, nothing of great value was taken,' she continued, keeping the history teacher firmly in her sights. 'The thief, or thieves, broke into the library but fortunately the smoke detectors went off and raised the alarm. The fire brigade and police were here within minutes, however they weren't able to catch the culprits.' She paused.

'Was anything taken?' Jane Lindsay, the librarian asked, looking shocked.

'As I said, nothing of any great value. Only the old South American casket from the Reference Library.' Dr. Klinger turned to look again at Jonathan Ramshaw. His mouth was open and his face had gone pale. 'I don't feel there's a need to inform the students at this stage and I'm sure the news is of no interest to any outside parties.' Dr. Klinger smiled. 'I will certainly inform you if there are any further developments.' She nodded briefly. The matter was closed.

Dr. Klinger moved quickly towards Jonathan Ramshaw.

'Jonathan, a word in my office?' she said.

Jonathan nodded, picked up his cup of tea and followed the principal into her office. Morris Tate, the newly elected head of school council, turned as they entered the room.

'Jonathan, we are very sorry about the loss of that artefact of yours. Was it valuable?' he asked.

Dr. Klinger pulled out a chair and Jonathan sat down.

'Its value is incalculable,' he said, finally, his voice a hoarse whisper. 'But in itself, it is just a chest.'

The councilor frowned.

'And what exactly does that mean?' For the first time Jonathan lifted his head and looked into the eyes of Morris Tate.

'That means that to most eyes, the chest is just that; an empty wooden casket of no monetary worth. However ...' Jonathan paused, sensing the principal and councilor leaning forward slightly.

'However?' the principal said.

Jonathan felt a growing unease with the direction of their questioning. He'd noticed the principal had become more intense and short in her dealings with both staff and students of late. Ever since the return from her collapse.

'It is just a wooden chest,' he said, wary of their sudden interest. 'But it is of great sentimental value to me and I should like it returned.'

'But there ...'

Dr. Klinger interrupted the school councilor.

'Then it is very important that we attempt to locate this box,' she said, glaring at Morris Tate. 'Find the chest and return it here to its rightful place. Correct, Jonathan?' she smiled.

Jonathan nodded.

'It is very strange,' he muttered, shaking his head. 'Are you sure nothing else was taken?' he asked.

'Quite sure,' the principal nodded.

'What are you thinking, Jonathan?' Morris

Tate said, eyeing him closely.

'There are some valuable and quite rare books and documents in that room, including a page from the first printing of the Gutenberg Bible, as well as the Renaissance Italian jewelry from the Scatini collection kept there,' said Jonathan. 'Why wasn't any of that taken?'

'Why indeed?' Dr. Klinger said, evenly. 'Perhaps the thief suspected the casket held something of more value.'

Jonathan shook his head. 'Nothing of any note.'

'Don't you worry, Mr. Ramshaw. We shall find your South American chest. And when we do I shall be most interested in you telling us all about its mysteries. Perhaps the entire school council would be interested. What do you think, Dr. Klinger?'

'Of course, Morris. But first we must hunt down the casket.'

'I would think hunting down the criminals who stole the casket would be just as valuable,' Jonathan Ramshaw said quietly.

'Well, of course,' Morris said, quickly. 'That

goes without saying.' He stood up. 'I have a friend down at police headquarters. I'll see if they have any leads.'

'Thank you, Morris. I'm glad we have you on our side in this matter,' Dr. Klinger said, also standing. The school bell rang. 'Thank you, Jonathan. I shall certainly let you know the minute we have news.'

'Thank you, Deirdre. I would appreciate that.'

Jonathan left her office, his mind even more troubled than it had been when he'd entered just a few minutes ago. For a brief moment their eyes had met. There was something about Deirdre Klinger that was puzzling Jonathan, but he couldn't pinpoint exactly what it was. It was as if the extra layers of make-up she had recently taken to applying to her face were hiding something.

But what?

Amanda's Letter
— Part Three

13 SEPTEMBER, 10.38 P.M.
Lewis, lying beneath the covers of his bed, was convinced the storm was now directly over the school. Like a set of broken lights on a Christmas tree, the dormitory flashed constantly moving from a blinding brightness to darkness and shadow. On top of this howled a raging wind, buffeting the trees. Driving rain lashed against the windows.

But it was the thunder that most disturbed Lewis.

I woke up shivering.

I had slid down into a comfortable patch of long grass. Someone was gently pressing my arm.

'We must keep moving.'

It was Jonathan. He looked ghostly and pale. He must have noticed my shocked expression.

'The invisibility,' he said. 'It doesn't last. Not with me, anyway. Come on.'

Weak, aching and hungry, I slowly got to my feet. We didn't talk. Jonathan had much to tell me but I wasn't in a good frame of mind to be hearing the things he now knew. I trudged along behind him, silently rejoicing that every small step I took was one more step away from the fearful and terrifying invisible tribe.

Jonathan allowed me small sips of water and tiny bites of a strange biscuit-like block of food that he was carrying. We stopped occasionally and each time that I looked into Jonathan's face I was unsettled by his sadness.

Finally, late in the night, we stopped to rest.

'I think we have ventured far enough from their range,' Jonathan said, settling his large frame down at the base of an enormous tree. 'But we can only stop for a few hours. We are not far from the helipad.'

'Jonathan,' I said, as he tore off a piece of the sticky biscuit. 'What happened back there?'

He looked at me a long time. I started speaking again but this time he interrupted me.

'I will tell you the truth as I understand it,' he began. 'You are referring to the strange ceremony that took place, aren't you?' he asked.

'You saw?' I gasped. 'You were there?'

'I was, yes. They forced me to watch.'

'And did they do all that to you as well?'

'No. Perhaps they intended to, but I managed to escape first.'

'What happened?'

'I know quite a bit about this tribe. As much as anyone can know about a tribe that supposedly doesn't exist. I knew where to find the substance that would make me invisible for a time. At the old burial ground we'd stumbled upon. In the casket that Fraser had opened. And it worked. There was a similar casket, though smaller, during the *ceremony with you. That's why we're here.' He paused.*

'The ceremony?' I asked. I felt a knot of fear, deep inside me. Something had happened and I was about to find out. Jonathan sighed.

'I cannot be sure, but I think they have placed a curse on you.'

'A curse? What do you mean?' I sat up suddenly. 'What about my child?' Again Jonathan paused.

'The curse will affect you both,' he said, quietly.

'What effect?' I whispered, suddenly fearful of his answer.

'The curse of invisibility,' he said.

'What do you mean?'

'You will slowly become invisible.'

I let his words sink in.

'Are you sure?' I gasped, shaking.

'No, I am not completely sure.'

'But you think that's it. And my child?'

'And your child too,' he said, sadly.

My mind was spinning. I felt a wave of nausea rise up. Turning away I vomited up the disgusting biscuits that Jonathan had been feeding me. It couldn't be true. I refused to believe it. Time and time again

I looked at my hands. It was the dead of night but I was sure I could still see them.

'How long will it take?' I asked, finally.

'That depends on many things. To be honest, I have no idea. I won't know until you ...'

'Until I start disappearing,' I whispered, finishing the sentence for him. 'What if I never get to see my child?' I began to cry. Quickly my quiet crying turned to uncontrollable weeping.

Jonathan wrapped an arm around me and consoled me as best he could.

'I am so sorry this has happened,' he said. 'Believe me, I shall do absolutely everything I possibly can.'

He talked about me returning with him to Bridgewater, where he worked as a teacher. He would borrow a video camera and film me doing day-to-day tasks. He got quite animated chatting away about making a visual diary of me to give to you, Lewis. I felt Jonathan was my only hope in dealing with this strange curse and agreed to his kind suggestion.

With heavy steps and an even heavier heart, we pressed on, reaching the helipad a few hours later.

I recovered slowly in a hospital in Brasilia.

Jonathan was marvelous, managing to deal with most of the officials and government representatives we encountered with a quiet calm. He arranged the journey home and I was well looked after by the kindly nursing staff.

I was keen to leave the country behind me and begin the task of rebuilding my life as best I could. Although happy to leave, there was a place in my heart that ached for my husband, poor Fraser, whose body I had to leave behind.

I arrived at Bridgewater a few weeks later, dear Jonathan having paved the way for me to join the students in the boarding house where he was house master. I had trained as a nurse after leaving school and this was to come in handy. It was there that he produced Fraser's gear that had been shipped back from Brasil. Hidden inside a hollowed out reference book was the casket from the burial ground.

Oh, Fraser.

On that hot summer day when I first met Dr. Klinger — who thankfully approved of Jonathan's recommendation that I should become a live-in matron for the boys — you were five months old and beautiful.

I could see you and you could see me.

Every morning I thanked God. That first summer at Bridgewater seemed to last a lifetime. The memories of dear Fraser and the horrors of the rainforest had slipped to a tiny and distant part of my mind.

The boarders were delightful, the staff welcoming and Jonathan ever helpful. I had the wonderful grounds of the school to enjoy as well as the facilities the school provided for the students.

I swam in the pool, played tennis and socialized with the staff; bandaged cuts, attended to sprains and chatted to homesick boys. And of course, I looked after you!

Twelve, almost thirteen glorious years passed and we had all but forgotten the curse. Winters and summers, birthdays and parties. Holidays. You know it all; all except this secret...

And then one night, late in March, one of the boys asked me the most innocent of questions.

'You look pale, Ms Watt. Are you all right?'

I quickly recovered from the shock, dismissed the boy hastily, and then hurried into the bathroom to look in the mirror.

His words echoed over and over in my head as I stared at my reflection.

I stood in front of the mirror, gently running my fingers down my cheeks. He was right. I did look pale. The curse that I had all but forgotten was more horrible than I had ever imagined. Was it going to give me thirteen years with you then suddenly decide to remove me from the world?

My disappearance had begun. How long would it be before my body turned to ghost and then the ghost turned invisible?

'Lewis, man. Get up and check out the storm,' one of the boys shouted from the other side of the room.

The entire building seemed to shake as a huge clap of thunder cracked overhead. Someone had turned on the lights. Was everyone in the room awake? Hidden in his cubicle, the curtain for a door drawn across, Lewis closed his eyes.

Torn from the letter, Lewis realized that he was amidst the loudest, most ferocious storm he could remember.

7

Nothing Revealed

13 SEPTEMBER, 10.15 P.M.

Jonathan Ramshaw stared out his study window at the ovals below. It had been a fortnight now since the theft of the South American casket and there was still no news of its whereabouts.

The police had conducted their enquiries, interviewing staff and students alike. They had sealed off the Reference Library, dusted the area for fingerprints and searched both the buildings and grounds for any evidence of the thief's daring robbery. But nothing had come to light.

Jonathan Ramshaw sighed and turned back to his correcting, but his mind was troubled and he found it hard to concentrate. After re-reading the first two paragraphs of Luke Wang's essay about the Peasant's Revolt, Jonathan pushed the papers aside, stood up and walked back to the window.

Something deeply disturbing, perhaps even sinister, was happening but he couldn't put a finger on exactly what it was. The enormous changes to the school council were unsettling. There was Dr. Klinger and her sudden illness and the change in her since her return. And, of course, the theft of the casket. Were the events linked in some way? It had been a desperately worrying time, not knowing whether the casket had yielded its secrets.

And on top of everything there was always Lewis. After almost thirteen years the curse had finally reared its ugly head, forcing Amanda to leave the school. Not that the staff or students knew. Like Lewis, everyone had been told that

Amanda was taking well-earned leave while also assisting with the settlement of her late husband's estate overseas. It had been all that Jonathan and Amanda could come up with given the short amount of time they'd had to concoct something plausible.

Thankfully the curse had stayed away from the spirited boy.

To help Amanda as much as possible, Jonathan had worked hard over the years to ensure that Lewis remained comfortable and happy. Not so much with material possessions, but more with warmth, love and security. And Jonathan had been training him too. Lewis played a variety of sports and was fluent in two languages other than his native tongue.

Jonathan had even feigned an interest in electronic gadgets and his flat was full of radios, phones and an assortment of equipment that Lewis spent hours dismantling and putting back together. Jonathan wanted to ensure the boy had every available option at his disposal should a time come when he was on his own, perhaps fighting for his life. Jonathan's studies had taught him that invisibility was a gift as well as a curse. It was the one promise Amanda had demanded of him, if something ever happened to her.

And now something had.

'Prepare him for everything,' she'd said, time and time again.

Sadly, Lewis had never warmed to his love of birds, but Jonathan insisted that he be able to recognise every bird that Jonathan was able to imitate.

'When would I ever want to know what a scarlet macaw sounded like?' Lewis asked, time and time again. 'Or a hummingbird? Or a toucan?'

'You never know,' Jonathan always replied, smiling, whistling yet another bird for Lewis to recognise.

Not a day went by when Jonathan didn't look closely at Lewis for signs that the curse might have begun to take effect. In bed each night Jonathan mumbled a silent prayer of thanks as another day passed with the boy looking as vigorous and healthy as he always had.

Jonathan continued to research the Invisible Tribe in the hope of gaining some understanding of the curse. He spent hour after hour pouring over the manuscripts and books about remote and lost tribes of South America. For all the hundreds and thousands of words he'd read on the subject — including copies of the stolen notes written by Elizabeth Graham — only one passage had struck a chord. It had come from a dusty, dark blue journal that he'd stumbled upon in the basement of the Museum of Natural History in London. Over a period of three weeks he had copied the entire contents into five exercise books. But he didn't need his notes to recall the sentences that had struck him the moment he'd first laid eyes on them...

However, it would seem that the curse on an unborn infant will not be revealed until the child comes of age or suffers some severe shock or fright. Once activated the victim may drift from visibility to invisibility. It was thought that a strong mind might eventually overwhelm the

*process but the more usual outcome is that the body
will deteriorate and finally perish, the whole process
lasting only a matter of weeks.*

On his desk the phone rang.

'Hello?'

'Jonathan, this is Deirdre Klinger. I have
wonderful news. The casket has been recovered.
Would you please come to my office to verify
that this is in fact the chest that was stolen?'

'Yes, of course,' Jonathan Ramshaw replied.
'How? Do we know who took it?'

'I don't have that information at this point
in time,' Dr. Klinger replied, crisply. 'It seems
the police are keeping things very close to their
chests. But what's important is that the casket
is returned.'

'Returned?' Jonathan inquired. 'The thieves
brought it back here?'

'Perhaps we can continue this conversation
downstairs?' Dr. Klinger suggested in an even
tone.

'Certainly. I'm on my way.'

Jonathan switched off his desk lamp and
hurried out into the cold night air. The wind

had picked up and heavy drops of rain began to fall as he made his way across the oval. A flash of lightning lit the night as Jonathan entered the building and made his way to the principal's offices.

Dr. Klinger rose from her chair and moved towards a low coffee table where the casket now sat, as Jonathan appeared in the doorway. He was surprised to see the head of the school council with Dr. Klinger.

The wooden casket was the size of a small shoe box; a cat or small dog would fit snugly inside it. Jonathan approached it tentatively, the musty smell of the box reminding him of the rainforest where he'd found it, all those years ago.

'It doesn't appear to have been damaged at all,' Morris Tate said briskly. 'We haven't opened it. Would you care to check, Mr. Ramshaw?'

'Shouldn't we wait until the police have done their tests?' Jonathan asked.

'Our primary concern is that we have the casket back in our safekeeping.'

The Casket

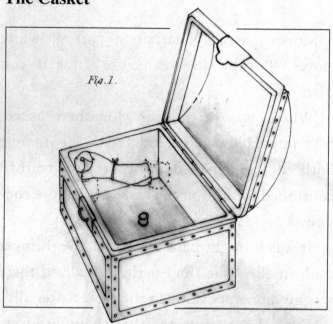

Fig. 1.

In each corner of the casket is a leathery **pocket** containing a potent
and concentrated substance representing each of the
four elements: fire, water, earth and air.

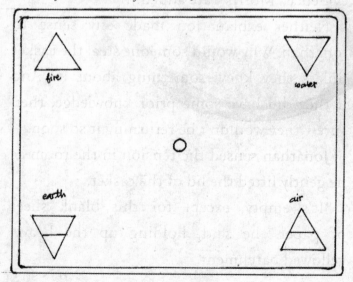

fire   water

earth   air

Fig. 2.

Morris passed Jonathan a pair of white gloves. 'But by all means use these if you wish.'

'Where was it found?' Jonathan asked, frowning. He was concerned with the interest both the principal and the head of council continued to show in the casket. What did they know?

'It was brought back to school,' Dr. Klinger said, finally. 'The thief perhaps realized there was no monetary value in the casket after all.'

'Or perhaps suspected that the police were closing in on him and wanted to be rid of the evidence,' Morris Tate added.

Neither explanation made any sense to Jonathan. Why would someone steal the casket unless they knew something about it? And if they did have some prior knowledge, then surely they wouldn't be returning it so soon.

Jonathan sensed the tension in the room as he gently lifted the lid of the casket.

'It's empty, except for this blank sheet of paper,' he said, holding up the heavy, yellowed parchment.

'Can you open that?' Morris said, leaning forward. 'How do you know it's blank?'

'It was there when I acquired it,' Jonathan replied, unfolding the paper. 'It is of no consequence.' He tossed the paper onto the table and quickly closed the lid again.

'Are you sure nothing's been taken?' the principal asked, moving in closer.

'The casket has always been empty,' Jonathan said, hoping his voice didn't display the sudden anxiety he was feeling.

Nothing could be further from the truth. All he needed do was put his hand into the casket to see if it really was empty, but he couldn't possibly risk that now, with the two of them standing so close.

Then again, if they knew its secret, why ask? Unless they want me to think they know nothing, Jonathan thought. He always felt that the safest place for the casket was in the library. Who would suspect something so valuable would rest in a place so public?

'Where did the casket come from, Jonathan? I am aware of your interest in the various lost civilisations of remote South America. Was it given to you as a gift, perhaps?'

'Not exactly,' Jonathan said after a moment, wondering where the conversation was heading.

Dr. Klinger, like the other staff members and students, had never taken a great interest in his collection of books and artefacts, few as they were. He didn't want to say he had stolen the casket.

'It came into my hands, though not via any formal ceremony or the like.' He paused again. 'Does the casket interest you, Dr. Klinger?'

'Not particularly,' she replied. 'Well, I suppose that is that. Perhaps you'd like to return it to its rightful resting place. I have also looked into improving our security measures. I think security cameras should be installed and we will update our alarm system too.'

'Good,' said Jonathan. He casually bent to pick up the folded piece of paper from the table.

'Shall I throw that away for you, Jonathan?' Dr. Klinger asked, holding out a hand.

'Oh, that's all right. I'll dispose of it myself.'

'A happy outcome then for everyone,' Morris Tate said, smiling thinly. But his voice was strained. To Jonathan he didn't sound happy at all. 'And you are quite sure that there is nothing about this chest here that has been tampered with?' he continued, following Jonathan out of the principal's office.

'Oh no,' Jonathan replied. 'As Deirdre suggested, the chest has no real value. It's just an interesting piece that I took a particular liking to.' Jonathan quickened his pace.

'Well, here you are then. Perhaps you'd like to return it to the library?' Tate said, holding the chest out to Jonathan.

Jonathan took the casket and watched Morris Tate walk quickly back into the principal's office, closing the door behind him.

'Working late, Mr. Ramshaw?' Martin Caldor said, pausing in his mopping of the floor.

'Bit of luck, Martin,' Jonathan said, nodding his head towards the casket. 'Can you open the library for me? I've left my keys up in my rooms.'

'Certainly, Mr. Ramshaw. That's your South American box then? Let's hope the police catch them.'

'Yes, indeed.' The cleaner unlocked the main library door then followed Jonathan towards the Reference Library section.

'Thank you, Martin. If you just lock the main door I'll lock up behind me on my way out.'

'That's all right, Mr. Ramshaw.' Martin hovered for a moment.

'There are a few other things I need to check,' Jonathan added.

The new head cleaner was a man Jonathan Ramshaw found very hard to warm to.

'Of course.'

Jonathan waited until Martin's footsteps could no longer be heard then opened the lid again, this time running his hand slowly around the inside casing of the casket. Almost straight away his fingers brushed against a padded pouch, like a pocket, attached to the rear left corner of the box. The pouch was there, but invisible. He moved his hand quickly to the other three corners where similar pouches were attached.

If only the thief, or Morris Tate or Dr. Klinger for that matter, had not just relied on their eyes to check the contents of the casket, Jonathan thought. For the casket was not empty, far from it. Jonathan could describe in detail just exactly what was in the casket.

In each corner was a leathery pocket containing a potent and concentrated substance representing each of the four elements: fire, water, earth and air. In the middle of the casket was an opening, a small cylinder, just wide enough for a finger to fit into. There were tubes running from the four corners, carrying their potent mixtures to the central point where, if you inserted your finger, you would become invisible.

Jonathan felt the familiar thrill of anticipation and excitement surge through him. Perhaps he could return to the principal's office under the cover of invisibility and listen to what was being said. Finding the narrow tube protruding from the center of the casket, Jonathan slowly inserted his right index finger inside. He gasped suddenly as an icy jolt of pain surged up his finger and through his body. It had been so long. He had promised never again to succumb, but now, without time to talk himself out of it, he had.

Suddenly he heard the sound of footsteps approaching. He closed the lid quickly, hurled off his jacket and quickly bent to untie his shoes. Curse the man, he thought, hearing Martin Caldor call from the library door.

'How long are you going to be, Mr. Ramshaw?' he said, now walking back towards the reference section.

Jonathan shoved his shoes and coat into a large drawer behind him and stood still. 'Mr. Ramshaw?' Every other item of clothing Jonathan was wearing was touching his skin. He was completely invisible.

The cleaner glanced about the room. The casket was where the history teacher had left it, on a table in the middle of the room.

'Mr. Ramshaw?' he called again, frowning.

There was no answer.

Again Jonathan waited for his footsteps to recede, angry with himself for giving in to the lure of the casket so quickly. When he was certain he was again alone, he opened the box, once more feeling for the tube.

This would be a burning sensation: brief, but excruciating. Closing his eyes he thrust a finger into the cavity. A searing, blinding, indescribable bolt of pain shot up his arm and coursed through him. It felt like tentacles of fire, travelling along every vein and artery in his body. But after a sharp intake of breath, Jonathan immediately felt the burning diminish to an uncomfortable tingling sensation as he returned to visibility.

As he bent to collect his shoes and coat a moment later, the pain had almost completely vanished. The pain was replaced by a rush of euphoria at having been invisible once more.

Jonathan waited another minute, unsure whether to move the casket. Would Martin notice it had been moved? Or would he wonder why it had been left on the table? Thinking that it would be safer behind glass, Jonathan raised the repaired glass panel and carefully lifted the casket back into its spot alongside the small white card that described it. He glanced briefly at the arrow lying alongside it. These were the only two artefacts from the invisible tribe. Perhaps it was now time to return them.

Morris Tate stared out through a window of the principal's office. The storm had intensified.

'Your history teacher knows something,' he remarked. 'I've never liked the man. He keeps things close to his chest.'

'You saw the casket, as I did, Morris. There was nothing in it, but that blank piece of paper. Still, I understand where you're coming from. We need him though. He is our only link to the invisible tribe. Above all, he must not suspect our intent.'

'We must search his rooms. He must be hiding something there.'

'No,' Dr. Klinger said, shaking her head. 'His suspicions have been aroused already. Patience, Morris. Rome wasn't built in a day.

We have the Crusaders now on the council. Ours is a position of great strength. Time, Morris, is not our enemy.'

Morris Tate turned quickly and glared at the school principal.

'Don't forget, Dr. Klinger, that it is I who am in charge of this operation,' he said, icily. 'I could remove the man now and ship him to South America. He is weak, Dr. Klinger, and weak people annoy me.'

'I will not answer to you, Morris,' Dr. Klinger snapped back. 'You know very well that neither of us leads this operation. My instructions come from Raymond Brampton, and I will be answerable to him and him only.'

Morris Tate held the principal's gaze then, sighing, collapsed into a chair.

'For such a significant and important operation, Raymond is very conspicuous by his absence.'

'Or is he?' said Dr. Klinger.

'What do you mean by that?' Morris looked up at her sharply.

Dr. Klinger shrugged her shoulders. 'I agree

with you. We are on the verge of the most startling development in human history and we should feel privileged that we are a part of it.'

Morris nodded his head slowly. 'Jonathan Ramshaw is the key. And, as I said at the outset, he knows something. If we don't act quickly, he'll destroy any evidence or links left to this tribe. Perhaps the boy knows something. We should use him to get to Ramshaw.'

'What are you talking about? The boy knows nothing.'

'What is the link between Jonathan and that boy? How did Jonathan Ramshaw suddenly come to be Lewis's guardian?' asked Morris.

Dr. Klinger sighed.

'His mother left the school some weeks ago. She was the matron at the boarding house.'

'And what? She just up and left?'

'It's not as simple as that. There was some talk of health problems and at this stage she is on leave. She is also attending to some affairs of her family — or so I am told. But you don't need to involve Lewis Watt. That would just be an added complication. He would know nothing about any of this.'

Morris Tate's mind was racing. Perhaps he'd get his own student contacts, Parker and his friend Mason Van Nuys, to keep an eye on Lewis. They were Young Crusaders now. The work would do them good. They were in the perfect position to monitor the boy. Morris Tate was a man of action and action was what he wanted. There was too much at stake not to keep moving. The history teacher could suddenly leave the school — just like the matron had.

Suddenly the lights in the room flickered.

An enormous clap of thunder crashed overhead. Dr. Klinger and Morris Tate ducked instinctively. Then the lights went out.

8

Amanda's Letter – Part Four

13 SEPTEMBER, 10.51 P.M.

For ten minutes Lewis lay curled up in a ball, his pillow and blanket wrapped tightly around his head and shoulders. Even then, white electric light and the deep rumblings of thunder penetrated.

But his mother's writing finally lured him out of his cocoon. Rolling over to face the wall, Lewis turned his attention back to the pages.

Lewis, I realise that I must return to the Amazon Basin. Return to the invisible tribe to plead with them for the curse to be reversed. I don't know for how long. A month, perhaps more.

Every day Jonathan took a photo of my face. The process is very gradual but after only a few weeks, when we lined up the photos, it was easy to see that I was becoming paler.

I am resigned to the fact that one day I will be invisible. Just when that day would come, we didn't know, but I have started preparing for the event. Deep down I know what I have to do, but I continue to avoid that option, desperately hoping that Jonathan will discover some miracle cure. He even travelled to South America during our mid-term break, returning with a collection of strange objects and concoctions, none of which made any difference.

Jonathan has given me as much information as possible. During these past few weeks, as my body ever so slowly vanishes from this world, I have studied all Jonathan's notes and maps; learnt some of the tribe's strange language. I have gifts for them, and I go with you in my heart.

I am leaving tomorrow. Somehow, some way,

I will return. Jonathan will take care of you. Of course he wanted to come with me, but I insisted that he stay and look after you.

I have a mirror on the desk as I write. My hand is pale, almost transparent.

I wear black clothes. Layers seem to help. Dear Lewis — why am I telling you this? Perhaps one day we shall read this letter together and laugh. We shall sit next to each other on a sunny day, visible to the world. Just you and me. Deal?

I remember once we had a storm, many years ago. You poor thing. You screamed and yelled. We couldn't find you. We looked everywhere. Suddenly it was very frightening. We could hear you, but not see you. Of course, we found you eventually — crouching behind Jonathan's desk in his study.

I have never seen Jonathan look so shocked.

'Lewis disappeared,' he whispered, picking you up from beneath his desk.

'Nonsense,' I said. 'He just ran and hid. He just vanished for a moment, that's all.'

'Exactly,' Jonathan whispered. 'Exactly.'

It is a time my thoughts return to often.

I'm not going to say goodbye. I shall return soon,

dear Lewis. I have just recently made contact with a man who specializes in face masks. I haven't told Jonathan about this. This specialist — he is the best in the world. You might just have to get used to your phantom mother in strange clothes, gloves and a mask, if I don't manage to reverse the curse.

We shall manage, Lewis. We have to. Jonathan, as your guardian, will decide when you read this letter, but I've just decided that I shall burn this letter as soon as I get back. That way I can tell you the story myself.

There is a candle on the desk here and its soft, yellow light glows warm. I look at the flame, Lewis and think of you. I am the candle, slowly diminishing and you are the flame, alive inside me.

I love you, Lewis.

Mom.

For a brief moment Lewis forgot about the storm raging outside. He lay still, not quite believing the final few pages. Why had Jonathan kept his mother's letter secret? Had he ever planned to show it to him? Lewis knew he shouldn't have been rifling through

Jonathan's desk earlier this evening, but he hadn't been looking for a letter from his mother. Just an eraser for his school work. Lewis peered out from beneath his blanket. Someone had switched the lights on.

Suddenly the curtain to his cubicle was flung aside and three screaming boys, waving their arms burst into the space beside his bed.

'We're going to die!' one of them screeched, dramatically.

Someone shrieked with laughter.

'Lewis, save us.'

'Wake up, Lewis! Wake up!'

A thundering explosion sent the three boys scurrying from Lewis's cubicle, this time genuinely frightened.

Startled, Lewis cried out, dropping the letter. Beside his bed, sheets of paper fluttered to the floor. As the last sheet hit the ground, another cracking blast drowned out the cries of the students, shattering windows along the north wall of the room. The lights flickered then the entire school was plunged into darkness.

Lewis stood rigid, frozen in fear. Lightning flashed for several seconds. Lewis could see his surroundings reflected in the mirror above his bed. Strangely, though, he could not see himself.

9

The Disappearance
of Lewis Watt

13 SEPTEMBER, 10.53 P.M.

Hidden away as he was in the library, Jonathan hadn't been aware of the sudden frenzy of storm activity raging overhead.

But within a few seconds of stepping outside he was drenched as he struggled against the howling wind blowing across the oval.

Lewis, he thought suddenly, trying to quicken

his pace. At that moment the entire building in front of him lit up as a thunderous explosion shook the ground. Jonathan stumbled, aware of a blinding flash behind the building. A few seconds later an enormous explosion shook the air. Street lights blinked and then suddenly the entire world was black.

'Lewis!' he shouted moving to the main entrance.

Groups of students were hurrying down the stairs, gathering in the main common room on the ground floor.

'Ring the bell!' he shouted to a student near the door.

Jonathan bounded up the stairs. 'Everyone into the common room,' he yelled.

The students knew the drill. Everyone was awake and carefully making their way down to the floor below.

'Have you seen Lewis?' Jonathan asked a student at the door of his dormitory.

'There's no one in here,' the student replied.

'Well done. Go downstairs.'

Jonathan stepped into the dormitory. A flash of lightning lit the room. 'Lewis?' There was no reply. Jonathan walked quickly to Lewis's cubicle and peered in. Another lightning strike illuminated the room.

Jonathan froze. Spread out on the floor at his feet were sheets of paper that he recognized instantly. Moving forward quickly he bent down to gather up the pages.

'Oh, no,' he whispered, standing.

Sweeping his hand beneath Lewis's bed, Jonathan gathered up the remaining sheets and stumbled outside.

Back downstairs, the students had gathered in the common room, chatting excitedly and waving flashlight beams across the room.

'Silence!' Jonathan boomed. 'Move away from the windows. I'm going to take the roll.'

Wiping rain and perspiration from his forehead, Jonathan began reading down the list of names — his calm, authoritative voice hiding his fear that he would be greeted by silence when he got to Lewis's name.

'Thomas?'

'Here.'

'Vu?'

'Yes.'

'Watt?'

No one spoke.

'Lewis, are you here?'

The students looked about.

'He was in his bed just before,' someone called.

'Are you sure? How do you know this?' Jonathan was trying to sound calm.

'Well, he was the only one who hadn't got up to watch the storm. So we sort of burst in to his cubicle and...' The boy's voice trailed off.

'And what?' Jonathan glared at the student.

'We just kind of woke him up, that's all.'

'And then what happened?' Jonathan asked.

'Nothing. There was that huge bang, the lights went out and so we came down here like you told us to, Mr. Ramshaw.'

The other students were silent.

'Shall I go back up and check?' Nick Howes, a prefect, asked.

'Yes, Nick. Check all the rooms on his floor. And call out his name.'

He looked down at the names on his clipboard, but his mind was elsewhere. A storm. A frightening storm. The shock of the letter...

In that moment, Jonathan finally had to accept that it had happened. Lewis was invisible. The curse had established itself in poor Lewis, having remained hidden for almost thirteen years. Was he in the room now, staring at him as he read through the list of names?

'Welsh?'

'Here.'

'Zanotti?'

'Yes, Mr. Ramshaw.'

'Very well. We have one student that is unaccounted for. I want the prefects to supervise the moving of all students who are in a dormitory with broken windows. I want their mattresses moved downstairs.'

Thunder rumbled outside.

'The storm is passing us.' He hoped Lewis

was hearing these words. 'If you are hiding away in here somewhere, Lewis Watt, please make yourself known to me.' Some of the students sniggered. 'Get those flashlights on, and let's get this place organized. Be careful of the glass.'

The students left the room, beams of light illuminating the passages and stairways as they made their way back upstairs.

Jonathan Ramshaw stood still. Outside the rain had eased. He waited for the last student to leave.

'Lewis?' he whispered, straining his ears for a sound. In the distance a siren wailed. 'Lewis, you have nothing to fear. Are you here?'

'Mr. Ramshaw,' called a student from the doorway. Jonathan looked up sharply. Had the boy seen him talking? 'There's only one room with broken windows. All those students are on their way down here now.'

'Well done, Blake. Thank you.'

'Jonathan?' a small voice whispered behind him.

Jonathan spun round.

'Lewis?' He held out a hand.

Slowly Lewis reached out his own hand. Their fingers met. Lewis let go quickly.

'W ... what's happened? The letter? You told me Mom was on leave. Visiting friends. Organizing stuff. Where is she? What's happened to me?'

'I will answer all your questions, Lewis, and more. Please trust me. I can return you to your normal state.' Jonathan hoped his voice sounded calm and convincing. He had no idea whether the casket could help someone who had been cursed. 'You must stay with me now. Don't speak unless I speak to you. Do you understand?' There was no reply. 'Lewis?' Jonathan hissed, urgently.

'I understand,' Lewis responded, his voice edged with fear.

The phone in Jonathan's pocket buzzed. 'Hello?'

'Jonathan? Jonathan this is Deirdre Klinger. Is everything all right over in the boys' quarters?'

Suddenly Nick Howes burst into the room.

'I can't find him, Mr. Ramshaw. There's no

sign of him anywhere. He's vanished.'

Covering the phone with his hand, Jonathan nodded. 'I'm on my way,' he said to the student by the door. 'Keep searching, Nick.' He returned the phone to his ear. 'Yes, Dr. Klinger. All of the students are accounted for.'

'Good. A transformer appears to have been struck by lightning. The entire school is out at the moment, and much of the surrounding area. I've rung emergency services and they're on their way. Peter Hiskin and Martin Caldor are on their way over as well.'

'Thank you, Deirdre.' Jonathan snapped the phone shut, looking about for Lewis. 'Listen to me,' he whispered. 'I'm going to have to stay here for some time yet. Lewis, there is nothing wrong with you at all. Quite the opposite. Are you listening?'

'I'm listening.' Lewis's whisper was shaky.

'Good. I am fairly sure your invisibility can be reversed. Meet me back here in fifteen minutes. I'll take you to the library where the casket is.'

Lewis didn't respond.

'Lewis, trust me.'

'I've got no choice,' Lewis muttered. 'I just want someone to explain what's going on. And where Mom is.'

'Fifteen minutes, Lewis. That's all I ask. You must trust me.' Hearing a group of students approaching, Jonathan moved towards the door.

'There's still no sign of Lewis, Mr. Ramshaw,' one of them said, a mattress trailing behind him.

'Thank you for your concern, boys. I'm sure he'll turn up shortly. Bring those mattresses in.'

Jonathan moved towards the door.

'What can I do, Mr. Ramshaw?'

Martin Caldor called from the far end of the room, standing by the only other exit.

Jonathan froze. How long had he been there for? Had he heard their conversation?

Unable to control his feelings, Jonathan blurted out. 'That door is an emergency exit door, Martin.'

'And this isn't an emergency?' the cleaner

asked, smugly. 'I'll head upstairs and look at those broken windows,' he said.

Lewis stood nervously by the large windows watching, making sure he was well out of the way as students hauled in their mattresses.

He watched as if in a dream. It was as though he was part of a play, but with a silent, nonspeaking role. A piece of furniture. An object that couldn't talk. All he could do was watch. It was the strangest feeling.

Fear had his heart racing, otherwise he felt no different at all. If anything, he sensed he'd undergone some mysterious transformation that had actually empowered him. He felt taller, stronger.

His racing heart calmed. He wondered if the sensation of power was the reason he was feeling as relaxed as he was. Lewis knew he should be beside himself with anxiety at the fact that he was invisible.

Quietly he watched as his friends slowly settled down. He edged forward when he heard his name mentioned.

'So where is he?'

'It's sure not like him.'

'Yeah, but remember the time in science when we were doing that experiment?'

Lewis closed his eyes and grimaced.

'Oh yeah,' Sandy Crane said. 'We had that table resting on all those balloons and we had to stand on the table. And then Lewis hopped on and the balloons burst. The noise of those balloons going off was amazing.'

'Yeah and Lewis was as white anything. Maybe the storm got to him.'

Lewis recalled the time clearly. He'd felt pale and sick, almost dreamy. Not unlike the sensation he'd felt when he'd first heard the thunderous explosion right outside the dormitory window.

Were the two related? Had he become temporarily invisible that day in science, two years ago?

'Flashlights out, boys,' Jonathan called, walking back into the room.

'Any sign of Lewis?' one of the boys asked.

'He's been found, Sam. He's fine. He'll be

back with us shortly.'

Mr. Ramshaw walked out of the room, pausing just outside the door. The room behind him remained silent. Hoping that Lewis was following, he slowly made his way towards the front door.

'Can you hear me, Lewis?'

'Yes,' replied Lewis, falling into stride next to Jonathan. Lewis was ready to listen.

'Well, firstly I am sorry that you discovered the letter the way you did.'

'I was ...'

Jonathan held up a hand. 'That doesn't matter. I am more sorry that you had to find all this out for yourself, without me there with you. As to your mother and the letter...' Jonathan paused, wondering whether this was all too much for the boy. He appeared to be taking it all in his stride though. 'There's really not much more I can tell you,' Jonathan said, pulling up the collar of his coat against the cold wind. 'The letter is very detailed, as I remember.'

'And what about my mother? Where is she?'

'I have not heard from Amanda since she left, Lewis,' Jonathan said, solemnly.

'But she went back to the tribe, didn't she? Why didn't you go with her? You know about the tribe. You could have helped her.'

Jonathan paused as two emergency workers wearing bright orange jackets walked past briskly.

'Lewis, I wanted to, but your mother quite correctly said that you needed looking after. She and I were the only two people in the world who knew of the curse. I had to stay with you.'

'Were? So she is dead?'

'We don't know that, Lewis. But she and I are the only people who have a map that can lead us to the tribe. I was going to sit down with you and go through Amanda's letter.'

'I'm coming with you, Uncle Jonathan,' he said, so quietly that Jonathan barely caught the words. He froze on hearing the last two words. Lewis hadn't called him Uncle for over five years.

'Lewis, let's not be hasty. First thing's first.

I want to see you in the flesh again before we discuss anything else.'

They had arrived at the reference section of the library and the glass display case housing the wooden casket. Carefully Jonathan unlocked the glass lid and raised it.

'Lewis, quickly,' Jonathan said, opening the casket lid. 'Where are you?'

'Out here!'

Jonathan carried the casket back into the main section of the library.

'You must place your finger here,' he said, pointing to the center of the box. 'There's a cylinder, just wide enough for your finger. In then out. It will hurt, but don't worry.'

'Is that all?' asked Lewis, stepping forward. 'Then why didn't you do this with Mom?'

'Lewis, I did. But she was neither fully visible nor fully invisible. It didn't work. This casket will only be effective on someone fully visible, or someone fully invisible. She wasn't prepared to wait. But I also suspect that she would need the smaller casket that was used when the curse was placed on her. And that, of course, is with the tribe.'

'Then she should have taken the chest with her, wherever she went.'

'She wouldn't. She said she'd return if need be.'

'Mr. Ramshaw?' a voice called out.

'Grab the chest,' Jonathan said quickly under his breath then turned to see the cleaner Martin Caldor standing by the library entrance. 'Must you follow me everywhere I go?' he said, exasperated.

'My apologies,' the cleaner said, smoothly. 'It's just that the teachers up at the boarding house were wondering where you were. I said I thought you might be down here checking on your precious casket.'

'Yes, well I was.'

The cleaner glanced at the door.

'I'll go lock up then,' he said, heading for the reference section.

'That won't be necessary, Martin. I'll see to it myself.'

The cleaner continued on his path across the room. Jonathan stole a glance out of the corner of his eye. As he expected, the chest was no longer visible. 'Don't let go,' he whispered, then turned back towards Martin.

Lewis thought quickly. He knew what he had to do. The cleaner must not enter the Reference Library. Moving quickly and silently, Lewis got to the door just before the caretaker. He pulled it hard, sending it crashing closed. Startled, Martin threw up an arm to protect himself as the door banged shut, his arm saving his face from receiving the full force of the door. He staggered back, his heart pounding.

Martin cursed, straightening himself and shaking the door handle.

'There's a strong wind out there tonight,' said Jonathan smoothly. 'Well, your job's done, Martin. I'll follow you back to the boarding house. I'm sure there's a lot more glass to clean up.'

Jonathan watched the cleaner muttering and cursing as he shuffled out of the building. There was something about the man... Jonathan couldn't quite put his finger on it.

Some days Martin could be quiet pleasant but other days — well, he made the back of Jonathan's neck prickle in distrust. It was like Martin had a dual-personality. He certainly limped more on some days than others. Maybe the pain made him surly.

'Lewis, don't you ever, ever do something like that again, do you hear me? Do you understand?'

'Hey! I got rid of him. That's what you wanted, wasn't it? Otherwise he would have marched right in there and seen that the treasure chest was gone.'

'I could have explained that.'

'Well, then, why did you want me to grab the casket box?'

Jonathan sighed. It was no use. From all the information he'd gleaned from his more obscure monthly journals, Jonathan had to face an awful truth. Now that Lewis was invisible, his body had undergone a transformation. Lewis's senses and awareness, his ability to think and make quick, sharp and rational decisions, was heightened to an extent beyond his actual level of maturity.

'Lewis. Anything you can hold, or that is touching your skin, will also disappear. Thus, when you picked up the casket, it vanished from right there in front of me.'

'The same with my clothes?' Lewis said, suddenly remembering he was wearing only pajamas.

'As long as they are connected to you in some way, yes. If you were wearing a sweater now and none of its material was touching your skin, then it would be visible.'

Lewis shivered, though he hadn't had any sense of feeling cold, despite the dampness of the material now clinging to his body.

'What about the floor? Shouldn't that be invisible?'

'Earthed,' Jonathan said. 'Like the table here. And this chair. But if you pick it up…' Jonathan watched fascinated as the chair he'd just touched suddenly disappeared right in front of his eyes.

Or had it?

He could just make out its faint outline,

shimmering and wobbling as Lewis held it in the air. Perhaps it was too heavy. Of course he knew himself of the power one's invisibility had over smaller objects, but he was nevertheless amazed to see it happening with someone else doing the touching.

'Lewis, we must stop. Let us get you visible and then I have something for you to read.'

'Uncle Jonathan, what if I like it like this? What if I cut myself? What happens to the blood?' A watch clattered to the floor at Jonathan's feet.

'Lewis, please. This is not a game. It's a curse!' Jonathan regretted the word the moment it left his lips. 'Please, Lewis.'

Jonathan watched as the chair re-appeared and then the casket on the table in front of him. Slowly, seemingly of its own, the lid opened.

'There's just one more thing I want you to show you,' he said, reaching into his pocket and pulling out the folded piece of paper. He held it in the air. 'Tell me what you see.'

The paper suddenly disappeared. Jonathan

heard the paper unfolding. 'Well?'

'It's a map,' Lewis said, staring at the detailed drawing. 'It's got rivers and compass directions. Amazing detail.'

'What is amazing is that the map is only visible to anyone invisible. To someone invisible, this map shows the directions to the Invisible Tribe. To anyone else, it's just a blank piece of paper. But enough. It's time for you to return to the visible world, Lewis.'

'Yes, okay.'

Jonathan wasn't sure what he'd do if his plan didn't work.

'In the middle. A smooth cylinder. Can you feel it? You might feel...' Jonathan heard Lewis's sudden intake of breath.

'Oh, thank the Lord,' Jonathan sighed, watching enthralled as Lewis appeared gradually taking on form. 'Come along, let's get you back to the boarding house.'

'What if it happens again? It was the storm, wasn't it?' Lewis called, watching Jonathan return the casket.

He remembered the words in the letter.

His mother's letter. And then he remembered his friends talking about the science lesson.

'I think maybe I've nearly disappeared before,' he continued.

'I think you may have too. But tonight it was the storm and the shock of the letter.' Jonathan smiled again at the look of wonder and flushed excitement on the boy's face. 'It was enough.'

'I guess I'll have to wait for another storm.'

'I guess you will.' How much time does he have, Jonathan wondered, recalling the words he'd read so many years ago.

Once activated the victim will drift from visibility to invisibility. It was thought that a strong mind can eventually overwhelm the process but the more normal outcome is that the body will deteriorate in time and finally perish, the whole process lasting a matter of months.

10

The Lure of the Casket

14 SEPTEMBER, 08.23 A.M.

Feigning sickness, Lewis spent the next two days locked away in Jonathan's rooms. He pored over his mother's letter and listened to Jonathan reveal all that he knew of the mysterious Invisible Tribe. Finally, Lewis ventured back out into the school.

Lewis's world had flipped upside down and although Jonathan had tried to maintain a sense of calm and reason during their many conversations, Lewis had found it increasingly difficult to contain the excitement and anticipation bubbling inside him. Underlying this positive energy was a draining sadness for his mother's predicament.

Hour after hour, he bombarded Jonathan with questions about his mother, the tribe, the trip to South America and the casket. But there was one question that continually popped up in their conversations, again and again. Could Lewis make himself invisible?

At first Jonathan had gently tried to ignore Lewis, sweeping aside the question with a frown and a shake of the head. But Lewis persisted.

'Lewis, there are many things I am yet to learn about invisibility, but I believe that it's possible to train yourself to control your visibility.' Jonathan eyed Lewis carefully. This was perhaps his only hope of surviving the curse. Should he be told after all? He was handling the whole situation so remarkably well.

'Lewis, it is my understanding that now that

the effects of the curse have appeared in you, there are two possibilities.'

Lewis nodded eagerly, leaning forward and staring into Jonathan's eyes.

'The first is that you will, in time, learn to control the forces inside you and move from visibility to invisibility as the need arises.'

'So that...'

Jonathan held up a hand. 'No. As long as you're living here and working at school, there is absolutely no need for you to move from one form to the other, nor is there any reason for you to tell anyone about this. It is a deep secret, Lewis and must remain so. The knowledge of invisibility in the wrong hands is extremely dangerous.'

Lewis nodded, trying to hide the tingles of excitement flitting up and down his spine. Who would ever know, he thought. Not even Jonathan.

'And the other possibility?' Lewis asked.

'The other is far more serious, of course. It is why your mother is not with us at the moment.'

'You mean that I end up permanently invisible?'

Jonathan nodded, watching Lewis keenly for some sign of shock or fear.

'But that's okay. There's that casket. I just stick my hand in there and I'm normal again.'

'It's not that easy. Whatever that substance is in the casket, it is not limitless. It will run out.'

'So, we just go and get more. We just go back to the tribe and get another casket. We've got the map.'

Jonathan sighed, shaking his head.

'I wish it were that simple, Lewis. But it is the first option we must look at.'

'Well, how do I practice trying to move from visible to invisible?'

'I'm not exactly sure myself, Lewis. Can you remember how you felt when you became invisible during the storm? What was happening?'

'Like I told you, I was lying in bed, reading the letter, and the storm was happening. I was frightened. Angry and shocked. And then the

guys burst in on me and I just lost it. I freaked.
I think it happened then.'

'Did you feel anything?' Jonathan was
curious. 'Did you sense something had
happened? That you had changed in some
way?'

Lewis closed his eyes, trying to recall exactly
how he'd felt, but there was nothing specific
he could think of that might have caused the
event to happen.

'It was just the sudden shock when they
ran in,' he said, almost to himself. 'It confused
me. It was like being woken up suddenly
from a really deep sleep. Like going from
really hot to really cold.'

'Perhaps that's it,' Jonathan said, quietly.
'An opening in your thoughts as you are
taken from one train of thought to another,
without you choosing to go that way.'

'I don't understand,' Lewis said, looking
perplexed.

'I'm not sure I do either,' Jonathan replied.
'But it's something to work on.' He stood up.
'Anyway, enough of this. It's back to normality

for you, Lewis. And remember, not a word about this to anyone. You've just been sick these last few days. You've had a bug.'

'An invisible bug.' Lewis grinned.

Jonathan smiled. 'The worst kind of bug to get.'

'No, the best kind of bug to get,' Lewis countered.

Lewis got back into school life with a new found energy that surprised even him. Abby persistently asked if he was feeling better, what had actually been the problem, was it contagious. Lewis fobbed her off with excuses of just a bad cold.

During class and sport he tried to focus entirely on the subject, putting the experience of his invisibility firmly to the back of his mind, but as each day went by, it became increasingly difficult, even for just a few minutes, to avoid reliving the amazing feeling of being invisible. With invisibility came a sense of power and freedom that Lewis had never experienced before.

Away from his studies, and long into the nights, Lewis tried to revisit the moment when the change had happened, desperately trying to capture the essence of what he was feeling the split second the invisibility took over.

He read everything that Jonathan gave him relating to the lost tribes of the Brazilian Rainforest, hoping for some hint as to how he might rediscover the magical moment; that mixture of intense fear, excitement and shock that had all blended together to suddenly turn his entire body invisible. But nothing he did made the slightest difference. Time after time, the small square fragment of mirror that he'd 'borrowed' from the science lab reflected back a clear image of his increasingly disappointed face.

He tried re-reading his mother's letter, but the effect was totally different from when he'd read it for the first time, during the storm.

A week after his invisible episode, as he sat in the library with Abby, Lewis had an inspiration. I know what it is, he thought to himself. It's not a shock or a surprise any more that will make me invisible. He looked up as the door to the Reference Library opened.

The casket. Of course! If the casket could be used to turn him visible, then maybe it could be used to become invisible.

'Hey, where you going?' Abby asked looking up as Lewis jumped to his feet.

'Reference Library.'

'Why?'

'I'm bored.'

'Well, that makes sense. You go from the second most-boring room in the school to the most-boring room in the school. Go figure.'

Lewis smiled to himself and headed for the door. Two Year Nine boys left the room as he entered. It was now empty.

He'd never really paid much attention to the room before. It was lined with old glass bookshelves and cabinets. Each of these was mostly filled with ancient books, open for visitors to look at. There were rows of encyclopedias too, but these were rarely used.

The South American casket sat with a couple of other old-looking artefacts in a small cabinet just to the right of the door. There was an arrow, a long knife with a woven handle, and what looked like a collection of jewelry.

Lewis stared through the glass panel at the lid of the casket. He could almost smell the rich aroma of old wood drifting upwards through the cracks in the cabinet. What was it inside the casket that could turn someone invisible? It was the most amazing thing in the world and he was standing there in the boring little library with the secret only a few feet from him.

Why would Jonathan keep such a valuable treasure here? Then again, who would suspect anything so valuable in a room such as this? Especially as it appeared that the chest itself was empty.

Before the pain had swept through his body Lewis remembered the conflicting sensation of fiery liquid, and yet there had also been something solid that his finger had pushed into. Lewis looked across to the door then gently tried to lift the glass lid of the cabinet. It didn't budge.

'Lewis?' a voice called from behind. Abby had suddenly appeared.

'Hi,' he said, his heart pumping.

'Hey. Are you okay? You look a bit sick.'

'Sick?' Lewis said, his hand feeling for the small mirror in his pocket. What had he been thinking? He'd promised Jonathan not to even enter the Reference Library, let alone open the cabinet that held the casket.

'Wasn't that the box that got stolen?'

'Yeah. I was just checking it out to see what all the fuss was about.'

'And?' asked Abby.

'Beats me,' Lewis shrugged. 'Looks like just an old empty wooden box.'

'You sure you're okay?' Abby asked.

Lewis followed her back into the main library.

'I'm fine.' He looked down at his hands, stifling a gasp of surprise as he saw how pale and translucent they appeared. Maybe he'd got too close to the casket. 'I'm just going to the bathroom. Back in a minute,' he said, rushing quickly through the main part of the library. Even then an idea was forming in his mind. He knew Abby liked him, maybe liked him a lot. But what would she think when he showed her his invisibility? How amazingly impressive would that be?

Lewis stared at himself in the bathroom mirror. It was if someone had removed all the color from his face. There was no flush to his cheeks, just a whitish glow that spread down from his forehead to his neck. He gulped in a lungful of air and held his breath, watching carefully as a hint of red gradually appeared. The door behind him suddenly swung open.

'Hey Lewis, what ya doing?' a freshman asked, staring at him.

'Nothing,' Lewis muttered, splashing water onto his face and leaving quickly.

He spent the next two days and nights anxiously mulling over whether to attempt to use the invisible magic from the casket. He knew he could find the key to the Reference Library on Jonathan's desk. He'd only be borrowing it anyway. What harm could there be? He already knew that the casket could reverse invisibility. All he wanted to do was to look at himself in a mirror up close and see if there was anything to see. It would be over in minutes.

In these moments of supreme confidence it was all he could do to stop himself from marching then and there down to the library, but Jonathan's warning was never far away, reminding him of some unknown danger.

'Don't ever, ever go near the casket. It has a power that we have no control over, a power that can change lives, even destroy them.'

The debate raged inside Lewis's head until three overheard words spoken by a student in the cafeteria finally tipped the scales.

'Just do it!' the girl had said as Lewis was passing her in the line to the cafeteria. She was talking to someone else but Lewis took it as a sign.

He smiled. I was meant to hear the words, he said to himself, over and over. Surely the words were for him. Before he could change his mind, he raced back to the boarding house, ran upstairs to his cubicle and grabbed hold of his phone:

Hey Ab meet me in lib at 8 2nite, got s'thing amazing 2 show. LW

That night, while the students in the boarding house were studying, Lewis slipped out of the building carrying three library books. Finding the key had been easy. Lewis was almost disappointed that Jonathan wasn't more careful with such a valuable item. There was even a wooden tag attached to it with the words Reference Library written on it, with smaller keys attached. He looked at his watch. Would Abby turn up? He hadn't seen her all afternoon, nor had she replied to his text message.

There were only three other students in the main section of the library, each sitting at a desktop computer. Miss Sawyer, one of the assistant librarians, looked up and smiled as Lewis slipped his books into the returns shoot.

'Is the Reference Library open?' he asked, trying to sound relaxed.

'No,' Miss Sawyer replied. 'What were you after?'

Lewis had rehearsed his lines.

'I just needed to take a photo of a couple of the South American things. I'm doing a project on them.'

'Sounds interesting. Mr. Ramshaw will be pleased,' she smiled. 'But I'm afraid that the room is remaining closed until further notice.'

'Oh well, Mr. Ramshaw lent me his key. He was going to write you a note but then he got distracted so I just came down anyway.' Lewis hoped that Miss Sawyer couldn't hear his heart beating like a drum in his chest.

'Well, why don't I just give his office a ring,' she said, reaching for the phone.

Lewis cursed under his breath.

'Oh, it doesn't matter,' he said, holding out the key. 'I'll do it in class tomorrow.'

Miss Sawyer held the phone to her ear and smiled at Lewis. Seconds ticked by. Lewis felt cold prickles of sweat on his forehead. Please don't be in, he thought to himself, desperately. Finally Miss Sawyer replaced the phone.

'No answer.'

Lewis let out a slow gasp of air.

'Just a quick photo and nothing else, okay?' she said, finally, smiling at Lewis.

'Yes. Thanks Miss Sawyer. It'll only take a minute,' Lewis walked quickly towards the Reference Library looking at his watch again as he inserted the key in the door. Two minutes to eight. He glanced back once but there was still no sign of Abby. Before he could change his mind, he quickly unlocked the glass lid of the cabinet, then holding the lid of the casket open with one hand, slid his other towards the middle of the casket. Abby or no Abby, he was going to do it.

Almost straightaway a burst of searing pain shot up his arm. He was vaguely aware of a phone ringing in the main library. The glass on the library's doors acted as a mirror. Lewis could see his sweater, tie and shoes reflected but nothing else.

'The library is closing!' he heard Miss Sawyer call from next door. 'Hurry up boys. I have to lock up now! Lewis?'

Lewis looked up sharply. Why was the library closing now? It never closed this early. Lewis flung his sweater aside, quickly checking the rest of him to make sure nothing was visible. Shoes! He kicked them off hurriedly, pushing them into the corner of the room, out of sight beneath a small table. He patted himself down, comforted that he could feel his skin and clothes. Anything touching the skin was invisible, he remembered. His watch, the clothes he was wearing; all had completely vanished.

'Lewis?' Miss Sawyer was suddenly standing at the door.

Lewis stood rigid, staring at her intently for any sign that she sensed he was still in the room. But she looked straight through him, shrugged then walked out. 'Did any of you see Lewis leave?' she called.

Lewis didn't hear their reply. The casket had a shimmering opacity about it which matched his own body. He had turned the wooden box invisible. Would the large cabinet disappear if he touched it? A door? A wall? A person?

He glanced upwards as the lights overhead started to switch off. He put the casket back then held his breath as he watched Miss Sawyer re-enter the room. She closed the glass lid of the cabinet slowly, looking around once again.

'Lewis?' she said again. She bent down to pick up his jacket then left the room.

'Why do we have to leave?' one of the boys asked.

Miss Sawyer shook her head. 'I'm not entirely sure, but that was Dr. Klinger on the phone and she's asked that everyone report back to their houses.' She was holding the door open for them. 'Are you sure none of you saw Lewis leave?' she asked again.

'I didn't even see him arrive, Miss,' Richard Yardley replied, glancing about. 'Do you want us to check around?'

'No, that's all right.'

Lewis waited over by the magazine rack as Miss Sawyer once more came back to look inside the Reference Library. Sighing, she closed the door.

The other boys had left. Careful not to touch anything else, Lewis waited for Miss Sawyer to finish locking the building. He knew the entrance to the library could be opened from the inside. He'd been down often enough over the years with Jonathan.

Even with the lights out, Lewis found that he was able to maneuver himself easily to the main door. It was like last time, he thought, trying to still the growing feeling of power and excitement. His senses were heightened. He was sure of it. He could see things clearly that he shouldn't be able to see at all. Perhaps it would be the same with his hearing; and his sense of smell. Maybe there were as yet undiscovered things that normal people couldn't do, but invisible people could?

'I'm invisible,' he breathed, stepping out of the shadow in the corridor outside the library. He checked the glass of the library doors which should have held his reflection. But they didn't.

Lewis walked from room to room in a state of calm excitement. Remaining perfectly quiet he touched various objects, causing them to instantly disappear. For fifteen minutes Lewis wandered about the buildings and grounds, hidden from the world.

A door slammed loudly close by. Someone was shouting. He crouched against the wall, listening. People were entering the building.

Maybe it was time to return to the library and reverse his invisibility.

As he entered the corridor that ran past the library he heard voices and then footsteps heading his way. Instinctively he flinched, retreating back to the safety of a doorway, despite his invisibility.

11

The Black Car

14 SEPTEMBER, 08.41 P.M.

'What are you doing here?' a boy called out.

Lewis froze. Were they talking to him? Could he be seen after all?

'Going to the library if you must know,' a girl's voice replied.

Abby! Lewis stopped himself from calling out. He turned to see Abby walking ahead of two older students: Mason Van Nuys and Parker Tate. What were they doing here?

'Listen, girl. You'd better get out of here.'

'Why?'

'Library's closed.'

'It doesn't shut till nine,' Abby replied.

Lewis watched Abby quicken her pace, trying to push ahead of the boys, looming over her. He closed his eyes as the three of them walked straight past him. Abby pushed open the library door.

'What the ...' Mason said.

'You were saying?'

Lewis carefully edged himself along the wall, then started to jog lightly away from the library door.

'Van Nuys? Tate? Over here!' he called from the far end of the corridor. He watched as the two boys looked at each other then started jogging towards him.

'Lewis?' Abby called.

Lewis ran back towards her.

'Abby, it's me!' he whispered.

Abby let out a long piercing scream as she felt something grab her hand. Lewis watched in awe as her body shimmered, parts of her disappearing. She flung his hand away and burst away from him.

'Abby?' he called.

She'd dropped her pencil case. Pens, pencils and other items were strewn over the floor.

'C'mon, let's get that casket thing,' said one of the boys.

They rushed into the library and appeared a few moments later with the casket. It was only when the boys were heading in the other direction, kicking Abby's belongings as they swaggered off, that Lewis realized they were carrying the key to him becoming visible again.

'Wait!' he blurted out then froze as the two boys paused and turned.

'Move it!' a deeper voice called from in front of them.

Lewis recognized Parker's father, Morris Tate, shouting at them from further up the corridor.

'There's someone down there,' he heard Parker tell his father.

Lewis watched him pass the casket to his

father who was moving silently towards the two boys.

'Here,' Morris said, ignoring his son and passing him what looked like a small silver cell phone. 'Press this button if there's a problem and you need me out here. Otherwise this meeting is not to be disturbed, do you understand?'

'And we get 100 bucks each?' Parker asked.

Morris lowered his voice. 'Young Crusaders are always rewarded for doing a job well. Now, you know the routine. Keep this area clear, but no rough stuff, you hear?'

'Yes sir,' the boys said, grinning.

Lewis glanced inside the small meeting room as Morris opened the door. Standing there with his head bowed, being supported by another man was Jonathan Ramshaw. His face was streaked with blood. Lewis recoiled as he took in the scene. It took all the self-control he could muster to stop from calling out. Instead he bolted for the door, just squeezing through as it closed behind him.

The room in front of him was a hive of activity.

The man was roughly maneuvering Jonathan to a chair at one end of the table. But Dr. Klinger, standing by the window and talking on a cell phone, was doing nothing about it. The noise in the room quietened as Morris Tate placed the casket on the table. Then the door behind Lewis opened again.

Everyone in the room froze as a man with a walking stick entered the room. Lewis watched in horror as he approached the casket.

'Sit!' he said, in a deep voice full of authority.

Even Lewis found himself looking for a chair.

'Mr. Ramshaw. You have something to tell us?'

'Who are you?' Jonathan gasped, looking desperately at Dr. Klinger. 'Deirdre, what's going on here?' He was visibly shaken. Lewis couldn't take his eyes off the streak of blood on his face; but he appeared unhurt otherwise.

'Show the footage,' the man barked.

The room suddenly went dark and a large television screen flickered to life. 'I will not be

denied, Mr. Ramshaw. I have been waiting for
this moment for many years.'

'I don't ...'

'Silence!'

A picture suddenly appeared on the
screen. Lewis's heart lurched as he realized
what everyone else in the room were looking
at. His watched himself walk into the
Reference Library and move quickly to the
cabinet where the casket sat. Lewis stole
a look at Jonathan who was slowly shaking
his head.

Lewis's mind raced. He had to do something,
but what? Even before the thought entered
his head he suddenly found his legs carrying
him swiftly towards the television. In his
eagerness to get the casket open he had
completely forgotten about the security camera
in the Reference Library.

Lewis flicked the switch at the wall. The
television hissed and went black.

'What is it?' the man growled.

Lewis flinched as the man crashed his stick
onto the table. He stood up threateningly.

Almost bumping into Morris Tate who'd got up to look at the television, Lewis scurried away, pausing close to Jonathan.

'I'm here,' he whispered in Jonathan's ear.

Jonathan didn't flinch.

'I demand to know what's going on here,' Jonathan said, standing. 'Who are you?' Jonathan glared at the black-suited man.

'Mr. Ramshaw,' he began, 'my colleagues have been watching you for a number of months. You can imagine how our interest was aroused even further when a lady, I think perhaps known to you, came to us not long ago.'

Lewis froze suddenly.

'Of course, I didn't believe a word of her extraordinary tale at first, but I like to check everything that comes my way. And she did look, how shall I say, not quite herself.'

'Amanda? Where is she? What have you done with her?' Jonathan blurted.

Jonathan felt paralyzed with fear. He just hoped Lewis could show enough self-control to keep his presence secret from everyone else in the room. But the man was talking about his mother. What did he know?

Morris Tate continued fiddling with the wires near the screen.

'Mr. Ramshaw, I am the world's leading expert in face masks. Allow me to introduce myself properly. My name is Raymond Brampton. Perhaps you'd like to come and see some of my work at the Chalet de Sombras, Mr. Ramshaw — my little hideaway in the mountains. As a leader of the Light Crusaders, I have been pursuing a number of methods to infiltrate the darker elements of our society. Probably my most successful invention to date has been a seamless facial mask, completely undetectable. A mask made of synthetic skin, manufactured in laboratories in fifteen different locations around the world.

'Your friend Amanda was in need of one, and quickly. So I made a mask of her own face, to wear over the invisible form of her real face. It was my most brilliant mask ever and a perfect

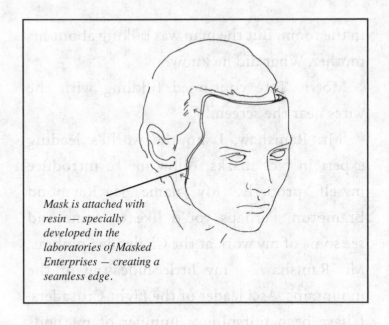

Mask is attached with resin — specially developed in the laboratories of Masked Enterprises — creating a seamless edge.

application. I only had a photo to work from. For beneath the mask covering her face was nothing.'

'Where is she now?' Jonathan snapped, horrified.

'All in good time, Mr. Ramshaw. There was something this lady wanted to do before she returned to the school here and to her son.'

The others in the room were leaning forward in their chairs, listening intently. Lewis leant against the wall, trying to control his shaking body.

'I was only too keen to help. She was indebted to me, of course. And she told me everything.'

Jonathan closed his eyes, and slowly shook his head.

'She had memorized a map, Mr. Ramshaw. A map that would take her to an invisible tribe, somewhere in the deepest rainforests of South America. So I sent her off with four of my very best Marine Crusaders. Two days into their journey, after landing them on a remote airstrip, we lost contact with them. We have heard nothing since, even though we have sent three missions into the area.'

'Why are you doing this?' Jonathan asked again.

The man ignored him. 'Mrs. Watt mentioned this casket, Mr. Ramshaw. Tonight, I am told, it has finally revealed its secret.'

'You don't know what you're doing,' Jonathan pressed on, buying time, wondering what Lewis could do. 'It's nothing but an empty box. It's an ancient artefact. Nothing more. Here, let me show you.'

Jonathan reached for the casket.

Once more the wooden cane cracked the table top.

'The switch at the wall was off,' Morris said as the television screen blinked. 'Perhaps there's a circuit breaker in there.'

Rolling black and white bars on the screen suddenly transformed into the unmistakable form of Lewis Watt, staring into the casket.

'You have done well, Dr. Klinger,' Raymond said, smiling.

Aghast, Lewis watched himself slowly plunge his finger into the casket.

'The casket, Lewis!' Jonathan shouted suddenly.

Lewis's mind suddenly cleared. He grabbed the casket off the table. It disappeared in front of everyone sitting around the table.

'The boy's in here now!' shouted Raymond, excitedly. He stood up again. 'Watch the door, the windows!'

The video footage was forgotten as everyone leapt out of their chairs. Lewis raced for the door, brushing Morris Tate.

'I've got him,' Morris yelled, grabbing Lewis

firmly. His body shimmered as he connected with the boy. Lewis sensed the others rushing towards him. Behind them the door opened.

'Stay out!' Tate yelled at the two boys.

'What's going on?' his son asked, before the door slammed shut.

Lewis swung his free arm at Morris's shoulders, tipping him off balance. Sensing the grip on his arm slacken, Lewis crashed his fist down hard on Tate's hand. He broke free and ran over to Jonathan, still seated.

Jonathan flinched as the casket nudged him in the side. Quickly he reached his hand into its opening, running his fingers along one of the tubes to the middle of its floor. He pushed a finger into the opening. A jolt of pain shot up his arm and he was invisible. Beside him, Dr. Klinger gasped.

'What's going on?' she cried.

The door had opened again. This time it was Abby.

'Stop!' The walking stick cracked hard against the wooden table one more time.

For a moment the room stilled, the adults

looking at the older man for direction. Abby and the two boys stood at the doorway, staring wide-eyed at the scene before them.

'Abby Fleet, go back to your house immediately,' said Dr. Klinger, staring at her intently.

In a flash Raymond had raced to the door, grabbing Abby harshly by the arm and dragging her into the room.

'Mr. Ramshaw, don't move. You and the boy are to remain here or the girl will not see the light of day.'

'You can't involve the students like this, Raymond,' said Dr. Klinger. 'Let her go.'

Abby screamed as she felt something cold and hard press against her neck.

'Nothing will get in my way, Deirdre. Not you nor your school.' He jerked her body roughly.

'Stop!' Jonathan yelled. 'Lewis, place the casket on the table. This has gone far enough. Neither the boy nor the girl has anything to do with this. Let them go and I will talk to you.'

'Wh...where is he?' Mason Van Nuys stammered.

'Do as he says, Lewis,' Morris Tate said, menacingly.

The casket suddenly reappeared on the table in front of Raymond as Lewis took his hands away from it. It disappeared momentarily then reappeared, along with Jonathan. Then Raymond snatched the casket up.

'Mr. Tate, kindly remove that tape from the player and give it to me. You have done well, Dr. Klinger. You and your school will be rewarded.'

But Lewis wasn't done yet. It was as if some unseen force was controlling his actions. He snatched the wooden cane from the table. It disappeared from everyone's eyes. Raymond yelled in pain as the cane smashed down onto his hands.

Grabbing hold of Abby's hand, Lewis charged for the door, sending a surprised Mason Van Nuys flying as he pushed him aside and burst into the corridor.

He hurled the cane to the floor.

'Jonathan!' he screamed, looking up and down the passageway.

'Lewis? What's happening to me? Is that you?' Abby cried.

Lewis felt a sudden drain of energy as he glanced at Abby. His limbs were going numb. Abby was disappearing, but slowly, not like the casket or the cane. Her face shimmered, drifting in and out of visibility. But the pain was getting too much for Lewis. He let go of her hand just as he felt another grasp his.

'Lewis, with me. Come along,' Jonathan said, gasping for air. 'The casket must be destroyed,' he added, under his breath. 'Make yourself visible and destroy the casket. I have the real secret in my pocket.'

'The girl!' Raymond Brampton cried.

Gritting his teeth, Lewis grabbed hold of Abby's hand again. She flinched but this time didn't cry out. The heaviness and numbness immediately returned to Lewis's body. The thought of running was almost too much for him.

Then a shot rang out.

'Lewis!' Jonathan called, stopping.

'Stop all of you!' Dr. Klinger screamed.

The two boys had fled. Raymond and Morris stood at the door staring down the corridor. Jonathan reached down, whispering to Lewis as Raymond raised his gun again.

'I don't need you any more,' he said, brandishing the gun, the casket held firmly in his other arm.

Lewis sprang to his feet and sprinted towards Raymond. Lewis slammed his head and shoulders into the man's stomach. Brampton gasped, sprawling backwards, his head banging against the floor. Lewis snatched the casket and sprinted back to Jonathan, who was now struggling to his feet.

'Jonathan, are you okay?' he whispered, trying to help him to his feet.

'Just a graze, Lewis. Open the casket. This must stop.' But before Lewis could get close enough, another shot rang out. Someone screamed.

'I had hoped it wouldn't come to this,'

Raymond Brampton wheezed, struggling to his feet. 'But you give me no option. It is over, Mr. Ramshaw. We are the Light Crusaders. I am here for the good of mankind. Have the boy reveal himself or I will kill the girl.'

'Lewis,' Jonathan breathed. 'Do as he says.'

Lewis glanced at Abby's terror-stricken face and reached for the casket. His body shimmered back into the real world as he slumped against the wall. A pair of hands locked his arms.

'Bring those three with me,' Raymond ordered, straightening his suit.

'I told you, the children have nothing whatsoever to do with this. Leave them alone,' Jonathan implored, pressing his hand to the knot of pain burning in his chest.

'Dr. Klinger, clean up this mess. I will be in touch,' Brampton snapped, walking away.

Jonathan and the two students were hurried outside and bundled into the back seat of a car parked outside the school. The driver carefully placed the casket in the trunk of the car then got into the front seat. It eased away into the night, the dark tint of the windows slowly turning black so that by the time they had got to the end of the street, it was impossible to see out.

12

Double Crusaders

'Invisible to the outside world,' Raymond chuckled from the front seat of his car with tinted windows.

He gave some instructions to the driver then turned in his seat. 'Now listen to me carefully, Mr. Ramshaw. You can save us both a lot of time by explaining to me everything you know about this invisible tribe and the casket, or you can waste my time and put your young friends' lives in danger. What's it to be?'

'Who are you?' Jonathan asked. 'How has the school become involved in all of this?'

'I've already told you, Mr. Ramshaw. I am the leader of the Light Crusaders. I am on the side of good. You have been keeping something secret here Mr. Ramshaw and it's time you shared your secret with the world.'

'It's too dangerous.'

'In the wrong hands, certainly,' Raymond said, nodding. 'The boy's, for instance,' he added, glaring at Lewis.

'Don't tell him anything,' Lewis blurted out. 'Sorry,' he added, turning to Abby squashed up next to him.

'Hey, I'm having the time of my life,' she said. 'Just remind me to never, ever turn up to an invitation of yours again.'

'Yeah, well I didn't know all this was going to happen,' he hissed.

'Oh, but we did,' Raymond said. 'You see, it was me that broke into your library to steal the South American casket. And it was empty!

There was nothing in it!' he started to laugh. 'Nothing but a blank piece of paper.'

'What's so funny?' Abby hissed.

Lewis shrugged.

'You are going to pay for this,' said Jonathan. 'Don't think you'll get away with it.'

'Oh, please,' Raymond snapped harshly. Turning slightly in his seat, he continued. 'So my good friend Dr. Klinger had that security camera installed. I leave no stones unturned, Mr. Ramshaw. I knew that the South American casket was central to this mystery I have been pursuing these past few months.'

'Yeah, well you didn't know...'

'Lewis, be quiet,' Jonathan said quickly.

'You were saying, my young friend?'

'Nothing,' Lewis muttered.

'The secret of invisibility,' the man said, more to himself. 'Imagine it! Just think of the possibilities. Think of how I can make this world a better place. My team of Light Crusaders will be able to infiltrate every organisation of darkness, every dingy hideaway. We will listen to their plans; we will know their movements; we will anticipate their every move. Slowly, we will eradicate the evil that exists in this world. We will start small, just as our founder did. A town, and then a city. A city and then a state. A state and then a country. And all the time we shall remain secret. No one will know of our existence.'

'Your intentions may be good, but you would be unleashing a power way beyond anything you could possibly imagine,' Jonathan said.

'Mr. Ramshaw, you could be my number one adviser. I can give you undreamed of power. We can form an alliance to fight and destroy the thieves, murderers and criminal networks across this country.'

Jonathan nodded slowly, believing none of Brampton's words. 'I will talk with you only when these two are returned to school and you promise that they will never be involved again in any of this.'

'Hang on a minute!' Lewis called.

'Lewis, enough!' Jonathan snapped.

For a moment Jonathan thought he had

gone too far, but finally Raymond nodded, said something to his driver and took out his phone.

'You are right, of course. We have no need for them, now that you, Mr. Ramshaw, have seen the merit of my ways.'

A dark, heavy screen separating the front seats from the back rose up from the floor near their feet, locking into place as it touched the roof.

'What's going on?' Lewis hissed.

'What's with Dr. Klinger?' added Abby. 'We should get the police in. She's gone crazy. Did you see how she did nothing to stop any of that? He had a gun!'

'Quiet, both of you,' Jonathan said, holding up a hand. 'Listen to me carefully. You are being returned to school. Do not speak to Dr. Klinger unless you have to. Return to your rooms and say nothing. Do you understand?'

'You expect us to just carry on ...'

'Abigail,' Jonathan said sternly, turning on her sharply. 'You have no choice. I'm sorry.

I will be in touch as soon as I return. Will you promise me to do and say nothing until I get back?'

Each of them muttered their agreement.

'Trust me, both of you.'

Raymond smiled as he listened through a small speaker to the conversation going on behind him. As the car sped quietly along the tree-lined streets of Bridgewater he thought about Jonathan Ramshaw. He was a sly old bird there was no doubt, but he would do nothing to jeopardize the well-being of his pupils and the school.

The two children, of course, would have to accompany them to the rainforests of the Amazon. But far better to dispose of them there. Raymond smiled as he recalled the fact that it sometime took only a matter of weeks for large mammals to almost completely decompose in the humid and putrid environment of the Amazon.

The car slowed. Raymond pressed a switch and took hold of a small microphone.

'Remember what your teacher said, Abigail

and Lewis. Speaking of this evening's events to anyone could have grave consequences for you both.'

'I will be in touch,' Jonathan whispered, ushering the two students out of the car. 'Trust me.'

'We've got no choice,' Lewis said, trying to see through the tinted glass to catch a look at the strange man in front.

'No, you haven't.' Jonathan closed the door and the car sped away into the night.

By the time the students had reached the front steps of Abby's boarding house, Lewis had told Abby everything he knew of his past. Not once did Abby interrupt. He told her about his mother and her adventures in Brazil; of the times when he'd almost disappeared; his fears of storms and loud noises and everything he knew or that Jonathan had told him about the Invisible Tribe of the Brazilian rainforest.

Abby finally said, shaking her head. 'I never would have believed it except that I saw it.' She paused, frowning. 'Didn't I? I'm not dreaming, am I?'

'No, you're not dreaming, Abby.'

'Well actually, I didn't see it. Or didn't see you. You know what I mean? That's so weird.'

'Weird spooky or weird strange?'

'Weird both of those things. Just weird. Lewis, things like this just don't happen. I'm heading off to the library to meet you for some reason, and the next thing I know I'm staring at a gun, a room full of mysterious people, a wooden box that makes people turn invisible and all the while my principal is standing there doing nothing. Like she's in on the whole thing.'

'Abby, she is in on the whole thing.'

'In on what?'

'The Light Crusaders. She's a Crusader.'

'So what is a Crusader?'

Lewis sat on the front step and picked up a small stick and started scratching the dirt with it. He glanced at his watch. 'I'm good till ten, what about you?'

'Same,' Abby agreed.

Lewis began poking the stick into a crack between the steps. 'No one knows much about them. Jonathan looked up some old books. They were this society that tried to wipe out bad things and bad people. They wanted to rid the world of evil. You know, crooks and murderers.'

'Isn't that what the police do?'

'Yeah, but the police don't hunt down these people to kill them.'

Abby gasped.

'Kill them? Sounds like the real Crusades.'

'Yeah, well maybe that's where they got their name from. All I know is that they don't always go by the book when it comes to getting the job done.'

'Well it hardly makes them good if they're getting rid of bad people by killing them.'

'Jonathan said that it didn't start out like that.'

'No wonder they want the secret of invisibility,' Abby said, gazing up at the stars. 'Hey, you reckon if I put my finger in that wooden box I'd go invisible too?'

'Of course you would.'

'But how? How does it work?'

'Dunno. All I know is that you get this really weird and painful sensation of burning and ice and heat and...' Lewis was struggling to find the words to describe the feeling.

'Ice and heat? As in, it's so cold that it's hot?'

Lewis thought for a moment. 'There are these four tunnels that come from each corner of the box and they all meet up in this sort of cylinder where you insert your finger. It's to do with the four elements.'

'As in fire, earth, air and water?'

'Yeah.'

Lewis suddenly dug into his pockets, pulling out what looked like a miniature game boy.

'What's that?' Abby asked, leaning over to look. 'Oh, your tracking thingo.'

'I almost forgot,' he said, fiddling with a dial. 'I left a tracker in the car.'

'A what?'

'You know, like I said in my talk. I had this in my pocket. I dropped the tracker down the back of the seat.'

Abby leaned in closer. A small green dot was flashing to the left of a circular screen. Lewis pressed a red button and the screen changed.

'GPS tracking co-ordinates. It's linked to satellites. Gives you the exact location. Anywhere in the world.'

'I know. You already told us.'

'Watch.' Lewis pressed the button again. The letters and numbers flashed and then suddenly writing appeared. Kenworth Street, Nth. 42mph. 'The tracker's in Kenworth Street, heading north at a speed of sixty-seven miles per hour. They haven't gone far at all. Maybe they're just circling the school.'

'Great. Let's go ring the police.'

'No, remember what Jonathan said. We should wait.'

'Well, I don't trust that guy with the walking stick. And it's even worse that Mr. Ramshaw does seem to trust him.'

'Yeah, well I trust Jonathan. He's all I've got.'

'Not as long as he's with that Raymond Brampton guy.'

Lewis looked at Abby then suddenly jumped up. 'You're right. C'mon.'

'Where are you going?' she asked.

'Isn't the gardener's shed around here somewhere?' he asked, ignoring her question.

'Right over behind the long-jump pit there,' Abby said, pointing.

'Good. Here, you hold this. Keep an eye on where they're going.' He tossed the tracking device over to Abby and set off for the far oval.

Abby stared at the small display screen, watching it change. A few minutes later she heard the sound of an engine starting up. Startled she looked up.

'Oh, no,' Abby groaned, getting up and jogging in the direction Lewis had taken.

She rounded a corner to be confronted by a quad bike careering towards her, a grinning Lewis standing up in the seat.

'Jump on,' he shouted, coming to a screeching halt inches from her. He revved the engine.

'If you think ...' Abby shouted over the top of the screaming engine.

'Whatever,' Lewis shouted, roaring off,

leaving a trail of dust behind him. Abby looked nervously towards her boarding house. Two surprised faces stared out from a window upstairs but no one else had appeared.

She watched the quad bike complete a hair-raising 180-degree turn, spraying mud, water and grass everywhere before charging back towards her.

'I haven't changed my mind,' she yelled.

'I know. I need the tracker,' Lewis shouted, holding his hand out.

'You can't track and drive that thing at the same time.'

'So hop on!' Lewis cried.

Suddenly the door to the boarding house opened. It was the headmistress of the boarding house, Mrs. Belcher.

'Is that you, Abigail Fleet?' she bellowed, marching down the steps.

'Um ... I ...' Abby blustered.

Lewis shot out an arm and dragged Abby onto the back of the quad bike.

'Sorry, Mrs. Belcher. I'll be back,' Abby called.

'Abigail Fleet!' Mrs. Belcher roared, before being covered in a cloud of dust and dirt. Coughing and spluttering she stepped backwards, tripping on the bottom step. 'Get back inside, NOW,' she yelled, glaring upwards. A dozen faces quickly vanished from four upstairs windows.

Lewis steered the quad bike out along a narrow dirt track that wound its way past the soccer pitches then through the main school gates.

'What's the tracker say?' he called, glancing quickly behind him. With one arm gripped tightly around Lewis's waist, Abby managed a quick look at the tracker.

'Hang on, it's just changing,' she called. 'Morgan Street. North-east. Twenty-seven miles per hour.'

'Okay, hang on. I know where that is,' Lewis called, swinging the vehicle hard right.

A pedestrian jumped out of the way, swearing angrily, just managing to avoid having his feet run over by a pair of squealing black tyres as the vehicle bumped up onto the pavement. Lewis steered it into a narrow street, cobbled and crowded with speed jumps, tyres and ramps.

'No way,' Abby said, fearing she was about to be given a joy-ride through an obstacle course. Suddenly there was movement to her right. 'Look out!' Abby squealed, as a cyclist shot out from a smaller laneway.

Lewis accelerated hard, aiming for a large wooden ramp. The cyclist braked suddenly as the quad bike bore down on him.

'Lewis!' Abby yelled, closing her eyes.

Lewis leant back and pulled hard on the throttle, just as the quad bike ran up the huge wooden ramp, angled upwards. It flew into the air as the kid on his bike dropped to the ground, the wheels of the vehicle missing him by inches. The machine crashed to the ground, bouncing and swerving as Lewis struggled to regain balance. Abby hung on desperately to Lewis's waist as she slipped to her left, finally managing to haul herself back to an upright position.

Lewis yelled in delight as the machine sped

off. Abby took a deep breath then glanced at the dial again.

'Still in Morgan Street,' she called.

'Speed?'

'Seventeen. Hang on. Eleven.' She watched the numbers count down. 'Zero. They've stopped.'

Lewis slowed as he approached the corner, turning left carefully into Morgan Street. Half-way down the street, parked alongside a playground was a large, dark car. A man was leaning against a tree. Lewis could see the bright orange glow of a cigarette. Raymond and Jonathan Ramshaw were still inside the car.

When Lewis and Abby were released from the car, Jonathan had made up his mind to tell Raymond everything. He had no choice. If the words about the curse were true then Lewis was in grave danger. Jonathan could think of only one place that might save him. Perhaps the most dangerous place of all.

'There's something I need to explain about

Lewis,' Jonathan said quietly as he watched the two students run from the car.

The car moved away from the curb quickly.

'Mr. Ramshaw, I have no intention of harming those two children, assuming I get my way and you offer everything you have and know about invisibility.'

'Lewis, like his mother, has been cursed. His only possibility for survival is returning to the tribe. But finding their village is virtually impossible,' said Jonathan. He wasn't going to mention the map. It was the one ace he had left. And it appeared that Raymond knew nothing of its existence.

'So we can work together, Mr. Ramshaw. You can direct me to the tribe. I will leave you to your business with the boy and you shall leave me to mine.'

'And what exactly is your business?'

'You know nothing of my work or the influence I have, Mr. Ramshaw. But you have been frank with me so in turn I shall be frank with you.'

He paused to take a deep breath.

'You've been spending too many years with your head lost in history books, Mr. Ramshaw. We have hundreds, perhaps thousands of Light Crusaders wearing masks, masquerading as completely different people. We have children, as young as nine, taking on the personalities of their twins. We call them our Double Crusaders, Mr. Ramshaw. And they are everywhere. Do you understand me? Right under your very nose!'

'But why? What on earth do you propose to achieve? And where are the original people whose lives are being doubled?'

'Where indeed, Mr. Ramshaw? Now that would be telling. Let me illustrate for you. A thirteen-year-old Young Crusader in Milan doubled as the son of a leading Mafia criminal. We had been training him for this role for two-and-a-half years.

'For three months he was able to infiltrate the mob, revealing to us an extraordinary array of secrets: names, addresses, plans for criminal activity plus a wealth of documented evidence that could have been used to put away at least twenty men for life.'

Jonathan was intrigued. 'So you got the police in eventually?' he asked.

'Oh no. We deal with the whole process ourselves. From monitoring through to resolution.'

'Resolution?'

'It was a clean operation from start to finish, Mr. Ramshaw.'

'But what about the boy?'

'A thirty-second operation to remove his mask and he is once again a nameless boy, ready to take on another role.'

'But the original boy. What of him?'

Raymond paused, looking at his bruised knuckles. He rubbed them slowly.

'He was the necessary sacrifice, Mr. Ramshaw. His was a needless life anyway. He was brought up in a world of thieves and lies. He was destined to live his life the way all those round him lived. We like to think of it as a double advantage.'

'Life is sacrosanct, Mr. Brampton. There is

no justification for even one life to be lost in order to save the lives of others.'

'Oh but there is. You may never understand, Mr. Ramshaw. It's all about numbers. That is all. Numbers. He is not dead. He may have his uses.'

'I could go to the police now and reveal everything.'

'Yes, you could. And endanger the lives of Abigail, Lewis and, of course, Amanda. We mustn't forget her.'

'But she's dead.'

The car had come to a stop. Raymond spoke briefly to his driver who then opened the door and got out.

'You're a historian, Mr. Ramshaw. Surely you don't believe everything you hear and read? You are weak and sentimental.' Raymond smiled. 'I have the casket. We will go to South America and save your boy, Mr. Ramshaw. Abigail will have to come too. I can't afford the risk of leaving her with the knowledge she now has.'

'She has nothing to do with any of this.'

'That is not my problem, Mr. Ramshaw. Do what you have to do, but like it or not, she is now involved. And I will be watching you every step of the way.'

'I'm sure you will. A word of advice. Don't use the casket. It will curse you as it has Lewis You will enjoy a brief spell of wonder and then die because of your greed.'

'You expect me to believe that?' Raymond spat, suddenly tiring of the conversation, and tapping his cane against the window. His driver threw his cigarette butt on the ground and moved towards the car.

'That's up to you,' Jonathan said, quietly. 'But remember, my view of life is a little different from yours. Even your life, Mr. Brampton.'

Jonathan felt the man's eyes bore into his back as he opened the car door. Weak and sentimental, he muttered to himself, shaking his head. We shall see about that. For all the virtuous motives Raymond had pumping though his brain, convincing him that what he was doing was right and good, there was for

Jonathan one irrefutable problem. It related to the so-called Double Crusaders. And it worried Jonathan immensely.

What had happened to the original people before they had been doubled? Where were they now? What had Raymond and his band of Light Crusaders done with them?

'Someone's getting out,' Abby whispered.

Lewis had maneuvered the quad bike behind a large bush by a fence, roughly thirty feet from the road.

'Hop off, Ab,' Lewis said, suddenly revving the engine. He nodded once, smiled, then careered away across the grass.

'Mr. Ramshaw?' Abby called, waving.

Jonathan looked up quickly as a blue quad bike came tearing across the park.

'Abigail?' he shouted, side-stepping the blue vehicle quickly. 'Lewis?' he gasped, suddenly noticing who was driving the machine. 'What are you doing?' he shouted.

'Tell you in a minute,' Lewis called, racing across the footpath.

'Lewis, stop that machine now!' Jonathan called.

'Lewis, stop!' Abby shouted.

Reluctantly Lewis slowed the machine.

The black car was moving slowly away from the curb as Jonathan moved up alongside the quad bike.

'But the casket? You said it had to be destroyed?' Lewis swivelled in his seat and glared at Jonathan.

'And what were you planning to do? Sidle up next to their car and steal it?' Jonathan sighed. 'No, there's been enough hijinks for one night. I'm not sure my heart can take any more.'

'I left a tracking device in the car,' Lewis said, nudging Abby.

She held it out for Jonathan to see. Jonathan stared at the small screen.

'Whereabouts?' An idea was forming in his mind.

'Under the seat. There's no way it will be detected.'

'Let me take that, Abby.'

'Hang on,' Lewis interjected.

'Lewis!' Abby passed Jonathan the device.

'Now, I expect you to return that vehicle to where you got it from and then go straight to your dormitories, do you understand?' said Jonathan.

'But how will you destroy the casket?' Lewis persisted.

'Just you leave that to me,' Jonathan smiled. 'Now, you two have some explaining to do.'

Abby thought of Mrs. Belcher and groaned.

'How do you get on with Mrs. Belcher?' she asked, sheepishly.

'And the gardeners?' Lewis added.

'It would appear that I am going to have some explaining to do also,' Jonathan said.

The three of them set off for school.

13

Return to the Tribe

23 SEPTEMBER 12.25 P.M.

'I still can't believe you're here after what you said last week.' Lewis stole a sideways look at Abby. 'How did Jonathan convince you to actually come? What did he say? And your parents?'

Abby sighed. She'd already explained it once, as Jonathan told her she'd have to. They were three hours into the flight when Abby turned to Lewis. 'Well, Mom and Dad think

I'm on a school music trip. A school music trip sponsored by Masked Enterprises.'

'But you're not.'

'Exactly. Jonathan has fixed it with the music staff. Don't ask me how he explained it, but supposedly it's all okay. Anyway, he says I have to be here because you made me invisible. Jonathan thinks that there could be something wrong with my body and that maybe, if we meet up with this tribe, they might be able to cure me.'

'Curse you, more likely,' Lewis said. 'You read my mother's letter? It doesn't sound like the people in that tribe are into helping others.'

'Except that we're not going to go trashing their sacred burial grounds like Fraser did,' said Abby.

'Fraser. My father.'

Lewis shivered.

Abby stared past Lewis's shoulder at the wide expanse of blue ocean outside the small oval window.

'Anyway,' Abby continued, 'I was just thinking of all the stuff you've had to put up with in the last week. Not exactly your average week.'

'You can say that again,' Lewis said, finally. 'But there's something else. Something that Jonathan's not telling me. It's about this curse. I think he's worried about something but he won't tell me.'

'So your mom has been cursed by the tribe and sets off to try and find them with the secret map,' Abby said.

'Yeah, but she somehow hears about Raymond Brampton and his face masks and so gets him to help out.'

'Right. So they set off for Brazil to try and find the lost tribe. And get lost themselves.' Abby paused for a moment. 'You know what I think?'

Lewis turned to look at her.

'Jonathan must be feeling pretty bad about the whole thing. I mean he was the one that set off into the rainforest with your mom to go look for Fraser in the first place.'

'Well they didn't have any choice.'

'Like you and Jonathan don't have any choice now,' she said, softly.

Abby was right, Lewis thought. And Jonathan had said as much just last night. They could leave no stone unturned in their quest to find Lewis's mother. South America was where she had last been seen, so it was there that they had to start their search.

Lewis had managed to busy himself with all sorts of tasks over the past few days, desperately trying to avoid having to contemplate just what was happening to his mother. He turned away suddenly and stared out at the sea.

'Hey, did Jonathan ever tell you how he managed to get the casket destroyed?' Abby asked.

Lewis shook his head.

'I've asked him over and over. Just says he has a broad circle of friends and that the tracking device was a brilliant move by me.'

Abby put on her headphones, closed her eyes and settled back into her seat. Lewis nibbled at the muffin on his tray and finally put on his own headphones, hoping the movie would distract him from the mounting pile of jigsaw pieces spinning in his head.

Behind them Jonathan sat alone, wondering about the identity of the man accompanying their small travelling party. He was surprised that Deirdre Klinger had decided to join them, though she had made her links with the Light Crusaders clear enough. There was also Morris Tate. Jonathan had tried discreetly to ascertain whether the man was wearing one of Raymond Brampton's mask but found it impossible to tell. He felt in his pocket for the map then returned to his book, desperately hoping that his ninth read of *The Lost Tribes of the Amazon Basin* might reveal some snippet of information that he had overlooked before. He wasn't hopeful.

The flight to Manaus was long enough, but when Jonathan explained to Abby and Lewis that there was another 200-mile-trip ahead of them they rolled their heads and groaned. Both were exhausted.

'It's another flight, but I assure you it's better than going via the river. You'll get plenty of time in a boat as it is. Come along. There's our plane,' said Morris.

Lewis glanced out the window at a small red-and-white plane with twin propellers.

'Will it stay in the air long enough for us to get there?' he asked.

Three hours later they landed at Téfe airport where they spent yet another hour waiting before boarding a small, hired bus that took them in a southward direction on a road that soon turned into a muddy track.

The driver sat hunched over his wheel, chewing on a stale tobacco leaf, whistling an aimless tune.

Abby stared out the window at the changing landscape. Myriad rivers and tributaries were slowly making way for a denser forest landscape. Bulging gray clouds hung overhead. It all looked heavy and foreboding. What am I doing here? she wondered, looking down at her sweat-drenched shirt. Jonathan had warned them that the humidity could be as high as ninety per cent. The atmosphere on the bus was stifling.

Three rows in front of her Lewis tried to relax. He glanced across the aisle at Jonathan, sitting alone, his head buried in a small, tatty-looking book, then pulled out his GPS navigator. He flicked through the controls on the GPS, checking the temperature, air pressure and altitude. He had no idea if it would be of any use, but fiddling with it kept his mind alert and active.

A small speaker crackled to life above their seat. Jonathan looked up from his book.

'Your attention please,' Dr. Klinger said, still sitting down in her seat. 'In just under two hours time we will be arriving at our first campsite. Tomorrow morning we will take a boat trip up the Solimoes River. Allow me to explain to you just exactly what is going to happen. It is time for a little revelation.'

Behind him, Lewis heard Abby gasp, her hand clasped over her mouth. Lewis looked up quickly. Jonathan had stood up, his hands gripping the seat in front of him.

'What—?' he said.

'D...Dr. Klinger?' Abby said, wide-eyed. 'What's happening?'

'Sit down, Mr. Ramshaw,' Dr. Klinger said evenly.

Lewis stole a quick glance behind him. Even Morris was looking shocked. The man next to him just smiled.

'Don't believe everything you see,' the woman laughed, picking up the mask she had just peeled from her face and dangling it in front of her.

Lewis stared at it, mesmerized. He could still see the features on the face that looked so like Dr. Klinger; the sharp nose, the high forehead with the sweep of blonde hair. Lewis turned away suddenly feeling sick as the woman spoke again. Blotches of gum and synthetic skin residue were still stuck to her face, though she paid no attention to these.

'Your first encounter with a Double Crusader, Mr. Ramshaw. Or maybe not?' She tossed the mask onto the seat in front of her.

Abby couldn't take her eyes off the mangled

piece of flesh draped over the back of the seat; the face of Dr. Klinger. The place where eyes should have been seemed to be staring right at her. A wave of nausea passed over her. She rubbed a cold, sweaty hand across her forehead and swallowed. What was happening? The woman was speaking again.

'My instructions are clear. You will proceed by boat to a site whose co-ordinates have been predetermined. Once there you are to await further instructions. The two children will remain with the boat under guard. You will lead us to the tribe, Mr. Ramshaw. Any deviation from this plan will result in the untimely deaths of you and your friends here.'

'Bravo, Julia. Welcome aboard,' the man beside Morris Tate clapped, as if at a brilliant performance.

'But how...?'

'Enough of your feigned ignorance, Mr. Ramshaw. Destroying the casket brought you so close to destroying yourselves. But we know of the map,' the man continued. 'We could have taken it from you. You can thank me that we decided not to. I normally like to take the lead, but in this instance following you with your precious map was the wisest choice. '

The woman named Julia sat back down again. The bus driver stared ahead into the growing darkness, slowly chewing his leaf.

It wasn't until a fire had been lit and the campers were huddled around it that Jonathan was finally able to speak to Lewis.

'I should have realized what was happening. It all adds up now, of course; Dr. Klinger's unusual mannerisms, her voice; her quick temper. But like everyone else, I put it down to her accident.' While Abby slept, the two of them had gone out to collect more wood.

'But where is the real Dr. Klinger?'

'I'm not sure, Lewis. But right now that's not our worry. You must do exactly as these people say. Nothing else matters now but for our safe return home. Look after Abby.'

'Come along, you two,' Morris called, marching towards them.

'Morris, think about what you are doing,' Jonathan pleaded.

'Oh, but I have, Mr. Ramshaw. Many times.' Morris grinned. 'And it just gets better and better. We'll round up these savages and give them a little taste of firepower. That should frighten them into submission.'

'What are you talking about? You have no idea of what you're up against.'

'Don't let it concern you. You have one job and one job only. To lead us to this mob of weirdos.'

'You won't get away with this, you know,' Jonathan said, pulling out his own pocket knife.

Morris Tate laughed long and loud. 'Well, we shall see about that, won't we Mr. Ramshaw. You and your pathetic little books. And what's that? Something you've kept since your boy scout days?'

Abby was still asleep when the others finally bedded down in their own sleeping bags for the night. Lewis lay awake listening to the sounds of tree frogs and Howler monkeys, and the distant cries of some unknown animal, wondering if he'd ever get Jonathan and Abby out of this nightmare. It never occurred to him that it was someone else's problem to solve.

During the night, two long, wooden boats slipped silently into the cove fifty feet downstream from the camp.

14

River Attack

25 SEPTEMBER 08.11 A.M.

The morning was shrouded in mist and gloom. The air was still and oppressive, even early in the morning as the group made their way down to the water's edge. Through the fog, Lewis could make out the vague shape of a long wooden boat slowly moving towards them.

'Mr. Tate?' a voice called. The boat emerged from the mist, another one just behind it.

'Yes, that's me.' Morris Tate waved and pushed Abby out of the way as he scrambled past her on the narrow track. Abby swore under her breath. 'Is my crate of goods with you?' he called.

'Yes,' the guide replied. 'In the second boat.'

'Good.' He turned to face the group. 'Mr. Ramshaw, I want you and those two in the front boat,' he said, nodding towards Abby and Lewis. 'Julia, perhaps you can accompany them? I'll take the second boat and be following right behind you. Now give me the map.'

'I told you, it's of no use,' Jonathan said, shaking his head. Suddenly he felt the sharp edge of a knife pressing into the side of his neck.

'You showed us the blank version last time, Mr. Ramshaw. Very clever,' Morris breathed into his ear. 'I know you've got the map. Do you want me to shred you limb from limb in front of those kids there or are you going to hand it over now?'

Jonathan reached into the pocket of

his shorts and pulled out the yellowing parchment. Morris snatched it out of his hands and opened it.

'It's the same piece of paper that was in the casket, you fool,' he yelled, the knife in his hand quivering. He hurled the paper into the water. Jonathan jerked his head slightly causing the knife to pierce his skin.

Slipping his backpack off, Lewis ran to the water's edge and waded in.

'Leave him alone,' Abby cried, rushing up towards Morris. Cursing, he slowly pulled the knife away.

'Then you better have a good memory, Mr. Ramshaw,' he said, finally. He hurled the knife into a stump.

Lewis slipped the piece of paper into his pocket, grateful to Abby for causing a distraction. Only Julia had noticed but she didn't appear to care about a blank piece of paper.

Half an hour later, their supplies packed into the front of the boat, they were afloat on the river. At first they made good time, the current flowing freely and the clear water refreshing, but as they moved into smaller and still smaller streams, their progress became more labored. The water had turned to a brown color and the guide in the lead boat was constantly dodging low branches and floating logs.

The air was sultry and heavy and it was hard to see through the blanket of fog that moved around them.

Abby and Lewis shared water and food as they listened to Jonathan tell stories of his trips to South America. He was trying to lighten the mood. At first, Julia, the leader of the group, slowly sharpening her knife near the rear of the boat, had told him to be quiet, but Jonathan ignored her, continuing to speak in his quiet, gentle manner. The only sounds now were the soft lapping of the boat against the water and the sound of Jonathan's calm voice.

Hour after hour the boats forged ahead. The humidity was making Abby feel sick again. Her clothes clung to her body. 'How much further?' she said, taking a long sip from a water bottle.

'I don't know,' Jonathan whispered.

Lewis kept one eye on the GPS navigator, trying to follow where they were travelling.

Suddenly the guide held up an arm. The boat drifted slowly forward. A strangled cry from the trees to their left shattered the silence.

'Get down!' Jonathan screamed. There was a whistling whoosh of noise. The guide cried out in pain. From the bottom of the boat Abby peered up, horrified as the guide keeled over and fell backwards into the water, his hands clasped around the long shaft of an arrow embedded in his chest. Another arrow clanged into the side of the boat.

'Abby! Lewis! Stay down!'

Jonathan pressed Abby further down into the interior of the boat. With her eyes clenched shut, she lay curled up, her hand gripping the teacher's shirt. For a moment all was quiet. Behind them, Morris had wrenched open the large metal case and pulled out a rifle. He loaded it quickly and fired twice.

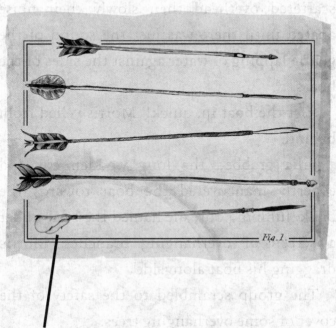

Fig.1.

Arrows found in the Brazilian rainforest. The arrow at the bottom of the diagram was identified by Elizabeth Graham as belonging to the Invisible Tribe in her detailed notes. (See also File no. 988776.43 Tribes of the Amazon Basin)

Lewis held his breath, cramped beneath the seat he'd been sitting on a moment ago. Birds scattered overhead then slowly their noise abated until there was just the sound of the gentle lapping of water against the sides of the boats.

'Get the boat in, quick!' Morris yelled from behind.

Julia grabbed the long wooden oar and expertly maneuvered the boat towards the bank. Jumping out, she hauled the boat under a screen of overhanging branches. Morris dragging his boat alongside.

The group scrambled to the safety of the cover of some overhanging trees.

'That's two men down. I'm going back to check on them. Wait here,' said Julia.

Julia moved stealthily through the undergrowth and hurdled back into the second boat. She returned a moment later, looking grim. The guide from the front boat and the unknown man who had accompanied them from the start each appeared to have been struck by an arrow.

For fifteen minutes they waited, alert for the slightest sound, but there was nothing to be heard but the occasional branch falling in the treetops overhead. The remaining guide sat hunched against a tree stump, staring fearfully at the arrow lodged into the side of the first boat.

'Mr. Ramshaw. You're the expert. Do you recognize it?' Julia asked, returning from her search.

'Of course I do,' he whispered, slowly levering the arrow out of the wood. He studied it closely, trying to conceal his surprise. It was from the Invisible Tribe, that was certain. 'But I don't understand,' he said finally.

'What?' Julia hissed.

Jonathan shook his head. From what he knew of the Invisible Tribe, daylight was their worst enemy. It instantly burnt their skin and affected their retinas, sometimes causing permanent blindness. They would hide from it at all costs. Something was wrong. But now was not the time to let the others know. A glimmer of hope flitted across his consciousness. He looked up at the others. Was this some sort of set up? Would the Invisible Tribe attack in daylight?

'This arrow comes from the Invisible Tribe,' he said, finally, not wanting anyone to think he suspected differently.

They stayed where they were for the rest of the day, too frightened to move away from the protection of the overhanging branches. Abby sat with her legs tucked under her chest. The gloom of the day lifted briefly and then suddenly it was night. The moon, slowly rising, cast an eerie glow in the forest beyond the campfire. Abby stared intently at the fire, avoiding the shadows beyond.

Finally, Jonathan stood up and crept slowly towards the boats. Abby looked up as he sat down alongside her, her face puffy from crying.

'Here, put these on,' Jonathan said, hauling two protective vests out from inside his pack. 'I didn't want to alarm you, but it appears we are much closer to the tribe than I thought. But something's wrong.' Jonathan lowered his voice even further. 'The tribe would normally never attack during daylight hours. But then again, I don't profess to know everything about them.' Jonathan sighed. 'All these people want are the secrets of the Invisible Tribe and all we have to do is lead them there. After that, nature will take care of itself.'

'What do you mean?'

'The Invisible Tribe will deal with Morris and Julia the way they have dealt with other white people trying to steal their secrets.'

'And what about us? What about Mom?'

'We will do everything we possibly can to find her, but you must accept that she may not be here.'

'I got the map,' Lewis said. It had dried quickly during the first part of their journey. 'But how will it help us?'

'It probably won't. But if somehow you become invisible then it can guide us to the tribe.'

'But aren't you going to take us there?' Abby asked, quietly.

'I don't know that I can, Abby. The tribe is invisible; their village is invisible; their huts, their monuments. Everything is invisible.'

'What about when you were here with Mom?' Lewis asked.

'An old ruin. Unused. A burial ground. We were close, and yes, it was visible.'

'What happened?' Abby asked. Quietly Jonathan recalled again the fateful trip he had taken all those years ago, his calm tone gradually instilling a sense of resolve and purpose in the children's minds.

The smell of food cooking brought the others back to the fire and for a while, Abby thought, they could have been happy campers on a night hike in a forest not far from home. But then Morris spoke.

'We need to start watches. I'll take the first watch till nine o'clock. You can work it out among yourselves who'll follow.'

He picked up the gun he'd left lying next to him and moved off.

'Just what is it that you propose to do?' Jonathan asked Julia.

'This mission has three purposes,' she said, her manner crisp. 'A fact-finding mission, to recover a casket and to bring back a sample of the tribe.'

'A sample?'

'One of the tribe members. Preferably alive.'

Jonathan snorted.

'And do you really believe that the two of you are going to outsmart a tribe that can see you clearly and yet cannot be seen?' he said, coldly.

'Not two, Mr. Ramshaw,' Julia said, pulling out a complicated looking two-way unit. A small red light blinked alongside a long, thin carbon-fiber antenna, extending from the top. 'Twenty. All armed and equipped and ready for some action. A force of the most highly-skilled Light Crusaders we have.'

A terrifying screech shattered the silence; a wailing, ear splitting scream so close that all of them jumped.

'Oh, what's that?' Abby said, covering her face.

'Lewis!' Jonathan called, staring in horror at

the place where he'd been sitting just a second ago. 'Lewis, are you there?' The vest he'd passed to him suddenly appeared in mid-air and fell to the ground.

'Mr. Ramshaw, what was that?' Julia called, hoisting her AK 47 assault rifle onto her shoulder and aiming it into the treetops. An arrow whistled past Jonathan's head, thumping into a tree just behind him.

'We must move!' Suddenly Jonathan gasped as another arrow narrowly missed his shoulder. Abby screamed as something grabbed her arm.

'It's me!' Lewis whispered, dragging her off along a narrow path that led away from the river. Behind them the assault rifle spat bullets into the surrounding trees, momentarily drowning out the screams. Foliage and branches crashed to the ground around them as Lewis and Abby burst into a clearing.

'Mr. Ramshaw,' Abby said, trying to turn back.

'Take off your jacket. Don't be seen.' Lewis stopped speaking, coming to a sudden halt.

'What?' Abby gasped, almost tripping. She

flung her jacket to the ground and looked down. She felt Lewis's hand tighten in hers. 'What is it?'

'Oh,' Lewis mumbled, starting to walk backwards slowly. 'I think I can see them.'

Abby was desperately trying to kick her shoes off. 'Who?' Beside him Abby disappeared. 'Oh,' she whispered. 'They're right there.'

Behind him, Lewis could hear Morris shouting into his two-way radio. There was another burst of gunfire and an awful wailing sound. Had one of the tribe been hit?

'There are three of them,' Lewis whispered. 'They're staring at us.' Lewis took another step back. 'It's the Invisible Tribe.'

He had never felt so frightened in his life.

'Lewis? Abby?' Julia yelled. 'Where are you?'

'Can they see us?' Abby's voice was barely a whisper.

Lewis didn't reply. In the darkness he could just see the outlines of their bodies, glistening with sweat. He watched in horror as the tallest of them raised his arms. There was something in his hands. A bow?

'Run!' he shouted, pulling Abby harshly away towards the trees. With one arm up to protect his face, Lewis dragged Abby ducking and weaving into the forest. They ran on blindly, crashing through the dense rainforest. Branches tore at their clothes and skin. Behind them, the screams and shouts started up again. Suddenly a vision of his mother flashed into his mind. Was he running on the same path she had?

Back near the fire, Julia stood alone, aimed her assault rifle into the treetops and let off another round of bullets. The screaming noises stopped abruptly.

'Come on, Abby,' Lewis gasped, dodging yet another enormous tree. Somehow he'd found himself on a track. The two followed it until Abby could run no further.

'Wait up,' she panted, hands on her knees. His heart pumping, Lewis let go of her hand and watched her slowly materialize. The drag and tiredness he'd felt when he'd held her back at school was not as bad this time. In the distance they could hear shouting. They both paused. There was another noise. A deep rumbling, gradually getting louder.

'What is it?' Abby asked, looking back.

'Sounds like an engine.'

'Maybe it's the reinforcements Morris Tate was talking about,' said Abby, peering into the darkness.

Suddenly the shouts started up again. The sound of sporadic gunfire echoed through the valley. They sat huddled together for what seemed like hours listening to the activity down near the camp fire. A larger boat finally arrived. Julia and Morris had grabbed everything they needed and were hustled into it by some large, muscled men in uniform. The remaining guide had fled into the rainforest.

'Lewis!' Julia called, one last time.

Abby went to stand up but Lewis held her hand, keeping her by his side.

'They're going to leave us,' she hissed.

'And what about Jonathan?' said Lewis.

They heard the boat's engines rev again as it moved out onto the water. A moment later it was a distant hum.

'Abby, stay here.'

'No! I'm ...'

'I'll come back, I promise,' Lewis said, letting go her outstretched hand. 'I've got to go and find Jonathan. No one can see me, remember?'

'But, Lewis, the tribes people will be able to. If you could see them, surely they'll be able to see you.'

'Maybe. Probably. I don't know, Abby. Anyway, the guns will have frightened them off. I can't just leave Jonathan lying there.' Before he could change his mind, Lewis dashed back along the path, looking down once to check that nothing of him was visible.

It took only a few minutes for Lewis to arrive back at the campsite. There was no sign of anyone. It was as if he was staring at the set of a movie. Plates lay about with food still on them and the fire was low, but still crackling softly.

Jonathan was gone. Maybe he'd been hit by an arrow. Maybe he was hiding somewhere.

'Jonathan!' Lewis hissed into the darkness.

He closed his eyes and counted to five. There was no reply. Cautiously Lewis crept down to the river. The two boats were still tied together but the bags of supplies had been taken.

'Jonathan, can you hear me?' he called again, a little louder. Nothing. He had to get back to Abby. He turned and ran back along the path.

'Abby?' he called, a sudden fear gripping him that she'd been captured during the few minutes he'd been away. 'Abby?' he shouted, louder.

'Yes,' she whispered, 'I'm still here.'

'Jonathan's gone. We have to go look for him.'

'Okay. Let's go.' Abby jumped to her feet. 'You're invisible, we've got the map and we can't leave anyway until we find Mr. Ramshaw. But first we go back to camp and get all the supplies we can.' She wasn't sure where it had come from, but a sense of purpose and resolve had surged through her as she waited for Lewis to return.

Back at the camp, Lewis put out the fire and

collected the gear while Abby carefully loaded their packs.

'Make sure everything you're wearing is touching your skin,' Lewis said, zipping up his bag. 'If you have to become invisible suddenly, I'll grab your hand, just like before, okay?'

'I wish I could see you,' said Abby, looking in the direction his voice had come from. More than you can imagine, she thought, recalling what Jonathan had told her about the curse. Was this the beginning of the end for Lewis? Would he ever be visible again?

A map suddenly floated to the ground.

'The map!' she cried. 'Can you see anything?'

It disappeared again as Lewis bent to pick it up. Abby felt Lewis's hand take hers. The cool, fizzy feeling of disappearing once more swept over her. It was the slightest tingly sensation. Pictures and color on the map suddenly appeared.

'This is amazing.,' she said, her voice filled with wonder. 'It looks almost 3-D.'

'Here.' Lewis guided her finger across the dried paper. 'This is where we are, I think. And we've got to head that way,' he added, pushing Abby's finger up the map a few inches.

'How far do you think that is?' asked Abby.

'Only about 6 miles I think. It's a bearing of 145 degrees. You take the GPS and keep us on a course of 145 degrees with the compass.'

'That's the easy part,' she muttered, looking at the compass.

'What's the hard part?'

'What do we do when we get there?'

15

Invisible Boy

26 SEPTEMBER 03.11 A.M.

They set off with Abby in the lead. She was over being anxious or worried. In fact, she was almost looking forward to whatever fate awaited them. She knew there was no turning around until they'd tried to somehow steal another of the secret caskets from the tribe and find out what they could of the whereabouts of Jonathan and Lewis's mom.

At first the navigating was easy. There was

enough moonlight filtering through the canopy overhead for Abby to be able to just read the dial on the compass. But soon the rainforest they were trampling through became more and more dense. It seemed that every few minutes Abby had to lead them away at right angles to get around thickly wooded areas. And all the while was the frightful thought that they were being watched. The two of them jumped at every noise. It was almost worse than being attacked, Abby thought. Hadn't someone said the worst fear was the fear of not knowing? She knew exactly what they were talking about.

Behind her, Lewis kept up a constant chatter, reassuring Abby that he wasn't ever far behind. Once, when he'd stopped his talking for a moment, Abby stopped and swung around in a panic. Lewis, with his head down, barreled into her, sending them both tumbling to the ground.

Though neither of them spoke the words, in both their minds was the growing fear that they were walking further and further away from Jonathan, maybe lying beneath a bush somewhere, slowly bleeding to death. Or being set upon by some kind of wild creature. Was a snake slowly strangling his limp and unconscious body? A swarm of spiders crawling over his face?

After hours of walking, Abby paused. A soft light was slowly creeping into the forest and a variety of birds were still welcoming a new day.

'Time for breakfast,' she said, hauling the heavy bag off her back. Relief and hope flooded through her. Had they survived the night? Then she thought again of Jonathan and the others. Where was he? Maybe he was at the invisible village even now?

She put out an assortment of dried snacks and watched, fascinated, as a few of them suddenly disappeared. 'Keep talking,' she said, grabbing an apple.

'I can't, I'm eating,' Lewis replied, his mouth full of food.

'So you can eat if you're invisible?'

'Of course. Let's rest here a bit,' he said,

closing his eyes and leaning back against a moss-covered stump.

'Hey, don't you think it's a bit weird that we haven't come across any animals?' Abby asked.

'Maybe they've learnt that living next to a tribe of invisible humans is not the smartest move.'

'I'd be looking for a new home.'

For a couple of hours the two of them lay there in the quiet dawn, listening to the bird calls, the monkeys chattering high above them and the breeze gently whistling through the trees. Then suddenly Lewis sat bolt upright, his head cocked to one side.

'Abby. Did you hear that?' he whispered.

Abby opened her eyes and squinted. It was broad daylight and for the first time in three days she was enjoying the warmth of the sun on her face. She grabbed the food, shoved it into the backpack and scrambled for cover behind an enormous rotting tree lying a few feet to their left. A moment later she felt Lewis push in beside her.

'What's happening?' Abby hissed.

'Look!'

Abby poked her head up over the tree. In the distance, maybe two hundred feet away, she saw two men walking quickly. One appeared to be carrying a bundle wrapped in dark-brown material.

'Is that Morris?' she whispered.

As they watched the man paused. The other man had disappeared from view.

'Did you bring those binoculars?' Lewis asked.

Abby dug deep into her backpack and held them up in the air. Suddenly they disappeared. Lewis powered them up and flicked the switch to day vision.

'What can you see?'

'Yep, it's Morris, alright. Oh—'

'What?'

'I think he's got a kid with them. A baby. In a blanket.'

Lewis's mind was racing. An invisible child, kidnapped from the tribe. But why? 'I'm going after him,' Lewis said, suddenly, dropping the binoculars to the ground. 'Wait for me here, Abby.'

'Wait on, Lewis. He'll have a gun. Don't you think...?'

'It's our best chance yet. If there's any of the tribe left then we get in the good books by saving the kid.'

'Why aren't the tribe coming after them now though?'

'Because it's daylight. Remember what Jonathan said? They hide during the day. They avoid the light and the sun.'

'So if that wasn't the tribe that attacked us the first time by the river who was it?'

'Maybe it was some other tribe. I dunno.'

Abby felt a hand squeeze hers. 'Don't worry, I won't do anything stupid. If I don't think I can rescue him I'll come back, okay?'

'Okay,' Abby sighed.

The two adults had begun to move again. Heading for the river, Lewis thought, striking out on a line to his left. Perhaps the motorized boat was waiting for them.

He moved quickly and quietly, keeping one

eye on the pair as they crept furtively along the ridge of a small rise.

Slowly Lewis gained on them. He could now hear the baby crying as it was bounced along. The man in front, Lewis realized suddenly, was one of the guides who'd arrived with the narrow boats yesterday. He had a knife in his hand.

Keeping well clear of the pair, Lewis moved ahead, waiting for them to stop. Finally, at a small stream, Morris called out something and paused, lying the baby on the ground.

Lewis moved in quickly, trying desperately to avoid making any sounds with his own movement. He'd got within about ten feet when he noticed the guide pause, then suddenly jump to his feet.

'Who's there?' Morris called, picking up the child.

Lewis froze, assuming that the guide had somehow sensed Lewis's presence. The man was crouched low, knife extended and slowly turning. But it wasn't Lewis that had caused the guide to freeze. Lewis followed the man's gaze. Only a few feet above, wrapped around a low branch, lay an enormous snake. Its head was reared and it looked like a thick bundle of green rope, looped around the branch.

'Boa,' the guide whispered, taking small, tentative steps backwards.

With the guide distracted, Lewis charged in the last few feet, knocking the knife out of the man's hand. Lewis grabbed it quickly from the ground. The guide put up both arms as the knife disappeared from view, then suddenly made a lunge. From the corner of his eye, Lewis saw the snake moving with alarming speed.

Lewis jumped back but not before the man had a tight grip on his arm.

'Hey!' the guide called. 'It's the kid!'

Morris quickly took off as Lewis kicked his leg firmly up between the guide's legs. Crying out in pain, the guide dropped to the ground. It was enough. Lewis lashed out with his other foot, this time landing a heavy blow to his stomach. The guide curled his body to avoid further blows.

Hurdling the guide, Lewis set off after

Morris. But he didn't have to run far. Tate had tripped and was lying on the ground, his pale face frozen in terror. The baby in its brown wrap was crying, still clutched in his arms.

In front of him, an inch from his face, was the snake. It had uncoiled a third of its body from the branch and its huge mouth was wide open. Morris tried desperately to remove his gun from its shoulder-holster after hastily placing the baby on the ground.

In a flash, the snake uncoiled further, sliding down the tree trunk toward the baby. Without pausing to think, Lewis grabbed a heavy stick from the ground and swung it at the snake's head, smashing its skull. The remainder of the snake's body writhed about for another minute and then stilled.

'What's going on?' Lewis asked, harshly. 'Where's Jonathan?'

'Is that you, Lewis? Thank God you're alive.'

'Where's Jonathan?' Lewis ignored Morris's insincere relief.

'Listen to me, Lewis.' Morris got to his feet, the baby still lying on the ground. 'This child is just security. That tribe back there has captured some of my Crusaders.' He held up the two-way. 'And the battery on this is dead. Come on. We need to get out of here before they catch up with us. Where are you?'

Lewis had silently worked his way behind Morris who was now glancing furtively to his left and right. But then Lewis's foot snapped a small twig. In a flash, Tate swung an arm out, catching Lewis by the shirt. Lewis swung his arm down but Tate's hold was firm.

Dragging the boy towards him, he jabbed his fist hard into Lewis's stomach. Lewis curled over in pain, gasping for breath. It had all happened in a moment.

Unhooking his gun, Morris grunted in satisfaction.

'It's time you were dead,' he rasped, 'like your doddery old friend.'

Lewis felt the press of the gun against his stomach.

'Mr. Tate!' a voice called from behind a tree.

Morris hadn't even noticed Abby slowly creeping towards them. A slight relaxation of the hold was all that Lewis needed. He lifted his elbow up under Morris's chin, causing the man to snap his tongue between his teeth. With a yell of pain, Morris let go. Lewis locked both hands around the gun. With both pairs of hands gripping the gun, it swung into the air and started firing.

'Let go, you idiot!' he shouted at Lewis.

'Grab the baby, Abby!' Lewis yelled, kicking hard at Tate's knee.

Tate reeled back, his grip on the gun loosening.

But Abby had other ideas. With a huge stick she came at Tate, whacking him a thumping blow to the back of the head. Taken by surprise, Morris slumped forward. Taking hold of his shirt, Lewis threw him hard to the earth. There was a dull thud as his head collided with a raised tree root. He lay sprawled on the ground, unmoving.

'What now?' Abby said, picking up the wailing infant. Almost at once it quietened. To the naked eye Abby was holding an empty shawl, but the weight of the baby was real enough. Parts of the shawl that touched the infant's bare skin were invisible. Abby glanced briefly at the other man, who still lay on the ground, curled up and clutching his stomach.

'Is this kid from the Invisible Tribe?' she whispered.

Lewis had unhooked the gun from Tate's arms and glanced around quickly for the snake. But it had vanished.

'Let's get out of here, before another snake finds us,' Lewis said, lifting the child out of Abby's arms.

'Snake?'

'Snake.'

'Snake?' Abby repeated, going pale.

'Abby, we're in the Amazon rainforest. Snakes. Tarant...'

'Stop! What about Mr. Tate?'

'Abby, come on!' Lewis called.

Abby followed Lewis back to their bags at the tree. They packed up quickly and set off.

Their progress was slow but the sunlight shining through the trees was reassuring, especially if it meant that the tribe members would be hiding somewhere, away from the daylight.

By mid-afternoon, they had begun a steady descent, moving into denser rainforest again. Lewis paused suddenly, Abby almost bumping into him. The child in his arms stirred, then went back to sleep.

16

The Village

26 SEPTEMBER 05.11 A.M.

'We're close,' he whispered.

'How do you know?'

'Look,' he said.

Abby looked and saw nothing but trees.

'Look where?'

'Abby, right there!' Lewis said, exasperated.

'I don't see anything. What am I supposed to be looking for?'

Lewis held his breath.

'Lewis?'

'Of course,' he whispered, faintly.

'What?'

'The Invisible Tribe. You can't see it. No one can see it. But it's there, Abby. Two hundred feet away. Right below us.'

Abby looked again. She could make out a vague sort of clearing, but nothing else.

'What do you see?' she breathed.

'It's a large, flat semi-open space. There are four huts made of dried woven vines. Pretty rough looking. Sort of in each corner. In the middle is a clearing. There's a huge fire, but it's just black ashes. And there's a platform, like a table. Oh!'

'What is it?'

Lewis pulled out the night goggles and put them to his eyes.

'There are poles. Tall, wooden poles. All around the edge. And … and …'

'Lewis?'

'There are bodies tied to them.' Lewis turned away, suddenly.

'Can you see Jonathan? Can you …' Abby

stopped suddenly. Was he looking at his own mother? Dead and tied to some wooden stake?

Suddenly, from the corner of his eye, Lewis saw movement. Three tall figures, cloaked in the same deep brown material that was wrapped around the baby, walked into the middle of the clearing. Others soon joined them.

'Can you see them?' asked Abby.

'Where have they been?' Lewis mumbled, watching fascinated as more and more tribe members gathered around a series of stone pillars, set near the platform in the middle of the tiny village. Even from his position, Lewis could sense anger and panic in the movements of the people.

'What's happening?' Abby asked.

'I don't know.' He took a deep breath. 'This is it, Abby,' Lewis said, standing up.

The baby that had been so quiet was starting to wriggle and whimper.

'This time I'm coming with you,' Abby said, shoving the map and compass into a side pocket of the backpack.

'Okay,' said Lewis. 'But stay hidden until I call you. We'll head down to the hut right in front of us.'

'Lewis?' Abby said, reaching out a hand.

'What?'

'Have you thought that your mom might be down there?'

'I've been thinking of nothing else. But I'm not getting my hopes up. Come on, let's get this over with.' He bent down to pick up the baby. 'Let's go.'

Abby followed Lewis along a steep path that wound its way down towards a small stream that bubbled and gurgled. More than ever she felt the presence of eyes, watching their progress down the slippery track.

'Okay,' Lewis whispered, removing Abby's shirt from the child. He crouched down by one of the huts. 'Now or never.'

Hoisting the baby up high above his head, he strode out into the middle of the clearing. From her position by the hut, Abby stared into the forest, seeing nothing at all but trees and thick wet vines.

On the other side of the valley, eight Elite Marine Crusaders lay in silence, waiting for the order to attack. They had followed the two children then crossed the valley via a narrow ridge. From there they had split into pairs, their grenades, flame throwers and assault rifles at the ready.

Their leader kept his night-vision goggles trained on the girl. She was the key and she was leading them to the very core of the invisible tribe.

His instructions had been simple and though they hadn't come from Raymond Brampton, they were clear enough. Bring out one of the natives — alive. Otherwise, destroy every living thing within a radius of two miles and bring back every artifact you can find.

Well, he wasn't risking the welfare of his men for the sake of a few wooden bracelets or woven fishing baskets. Not after the losses they'd suffered already. If there was anything left after the area had been cleansed, then that was fine.

Silent step after silent step, Lewis walked until

he finally came to a halt, just a few feet from where the tribesmen were gathering in front of the stones. They were kneeling with their backs to Lewis, their heads bowed in some kind of ritual prayer.

He looked around at the poles nearest him. The rotting remains of animals long since dead hung around the poles, though he could smell nothing foul. And then he saw her. His heart lurched as he stumbled towards a wooden post, set back from the others. A pile of bones littered the ground, but somehow his mother's face had remained almost intact. Fighting off a wave of nausea he stumbled forward, then fell to his knees. The baby in his arms bumped its head against his shoulder and began to moan softly as Lewis crashed to the dirt. Lewis closed his eyes and yelled.

In a flash, he was surrounded by at least fifteen of the tribe, their spears aimed at Lewis's heart. One of them stepped forward slowly and took the baby from Lewis's hands. Then, suddenly, he was being pushed and dragged to one of the stakes. He felt a cold chill run through him as he cursed his captors. Then he grew totally oblivious to the commotion going on around him as the truth finally hit him. His mother was dead.

He didn't care any more.

Nothing else mattered.

Rough hands wound a coarse rope tightly around his arms and body. Lewis looked down at the bones and flesh gathered in the dust at his feet. Suddenly he snapped. He closed his eyes, looked to the sky and screamed.

'Mooooommmm!' His whole frame shook as enormous sobs racked his body. 'Abby!'

His shouting had momentarily silenced the voices around him. Then he heard another cry and suddenly the hands binding him to the tree stopped what they were doing.

Abby had rushed into the clearing and was looking around wildly. Suddenly, a pair of hands reached out to her from nowhere and held her fast.

Lewis watched horrified as Abby was lifted off her feet. She screamed and swore, kicking out with her legs. Then suddenly she went rigid and stiff.

'Noooooo! You can't do this!' he yelled, shaking his head.

Lewis felt someone grasp his finger and suddenly he was overwhelmed with a burning sensation racing through his body. Immediately he looked around. The huts, pillars and everything else of the village had vanished. He turned around, still bound to the wooden pole, though he couldn't see it. Everything was gone.

He stood frozen, as a hand rested gently on his forehead. Then something was pushed into his hands. It was a small box — a smaller version of Jonathan's casket. A man was yelling instructions in a curious, high-pitched blend of chirps and screams. The ties that had bound Lewis to the post were suddenly cut. He fell forward and stumbled.

Was this some sort of gift for returning the child to the village? Lewis wondered, looking around him desperately. Was his life being spared?

'Lewis!' a deep voice called, from somewhere away to his left. 'Help me! It's Jonathan.'

'Jonathan?' He stumbled in the direction of the voice, 'Is that you?'

A burst of gunfire erupted from the hill behind him and then a huge mound of earth exploded just in front of the hut. Lewis flew through the air, landing heavily on his side. Another explosion sounded nearby.

Suddenly the village was visible, ablaze with fire as the Crusaders stormed into the area. Night had suddenly turned to day as the flames from a dozen fires, fanned by a cool night breeze, rose into the sky. And as the village became brighter, the tribe members started to run away.

'I can see them!' Abby yelled, grabbing Lewis by the arm. 'And you!'

Perhaps it was the fire that was suddenly bringing everything into view — including the tribe members themselves.

'Quickly,' Lewis gasped. 'I think Jonathan's in here.'

He kicked open the flimsy door and burst in.

Lying on the ground was Jonathan, his head cradled in his arm, his hands and feet bound by the same twine that had held Lewis to the post.

'Where's your pocket knife?' Lewis wheezed, the smoke in the hut getting thicker. He put down the casket and held out his hand.

Jonathan muttered something, shaking his head. His eyes were glazed and he stared ahead.

'Here,' Abby said, passing Lewis her own knife before covering Jonathan's face with a shirt from her backpack.

She poured water from her water bottle over the shirt and then over herself and Lewis who was cutting the binds. They helped Jonathan to his feet. Lewis snatched the casket from the ground and the three of them lurched out of the hut just as another explosion ripped apart the sacred stones. A moment later the hut they'd just left erupted into flames.

'Hey!' someone shouted. A blast of searing

hot fire spat out at them. Lewis jerked his body left just as a tree exploded into fire in front of him. Hanging on, the others followed him up a steep path.

Gasping for air, they made it to the top. The rainforest behind them was a raging inferno.

'Jonathan, are you okay?' Abby wheezed.

'Face burnt,' he mumbled, pointing to his head. He kept the damp shirt pressed against his face as they stumbled and staggered away from the inferno. Shouts and cries from the village grew fainter and fainter.

'This way,' Jonathan muttered, pointing to a track.

Lewis and Abby followed him through a mossy glade that ran along the edge of a small stream. The three struggled on into the night, sometimes running, mostly jogging, further and further away from the burning village.

At one point, Abby bent down and picked up a shiny object from the ground. 'I think that's my hair clip,' she said. She rushed on ahead. 'Hey, we're here!' she cried, seeing the two wooden boats still tied together.

Jonathan paused. 'Go and check them,' he said, his voice muffled.

Abby and Lewis jogged down to the river's edge. Jonathan pulled the two-way radio from his pocket.

'Ready for pick up,' he said, quietly.

'Copy that,' a voice replied.

Abby looked up at the sound of a motor.

'It's the boat again,' she said, turning excitedly to Jonathan. Then she froze. Jonathan was standing, his arm outstretched, with a gun pointing directly at her.

'What are you doing?' she whispered, staring in horror at the nose of the gun.

'Finally,' Jonathan said, slowly walking towards them, holding out his free hand. 'Give me the chest. You can try to fight your way out of this mad hole. But either way I'm taking the chest.'

Lewis gazed in confusion at the man in front of him. Why was Jonathan acting so strange? Jonathan would never talk to him... But this wasn't Jonathan. With a sinking feeling in the pit of his stomach he realized they had just saved Raymond from the burning village. He was wearing a skin tight mask of Jonathan's face. In the darkness and confusion neither he nor Abby had noticed his slightly taller and younger figure.

'Raymond? Where's Jonathan?'

'The tribe did the job for me,' he laughed. 'At this very spot. How pleasantly ironic.'

Lewis glanced to his right.

'And don't think about throwing the casket away. Or would you like to see the girl die?'

But it wasn't the water that Lewis was looking at. He'd heard the faintest noise coming from the boat behind him. It was the sound of a scarlet macaw — the bird call Jonathan has so often bored him with over the years. It had come from the first boat.

'Put it down now!' the man roared.

Carefully Lewis stepped across to the edge of the boat and placed the casket on the stern. He moved back slowly, his hands above his head, careful to keep himself between the man and the small wooden casket.

He'd glanced into the boat and seen Jonathan. Without the bird call, he never would have known he was there. Behind him in the boat, Jonathan Ramshaw quietly reached out a finger and inserted it into the box. He squeezed his eyes shut as the pain shot along his arm.

'Move away from the boat,' Raymond roared. He walked silently over to Abby and stood by her. 'Very good. Well, here's a little surprise for you,' he said, stretching a hand over the top of his head, his gun still pointing at them.

In a flash he'd removed the mask from his face, peeling away the layer of skin. Raymond stood in front of them laughing as the sound of the boat grew louder.

'Well, thank you both for saving my life back there. You are, in your own way, a small part of history,' he said, cocking the gun. 'It's just a pity that no one will ever know about you. Except the crocodiles.' He laughed again, then raised an arm.

Suddenly a small pen knife was flying

through the air. It embedded itself in Raymond's arm, just as the gun fired. Abby screamed as a bullet whistled past her head. There was a loud cracking sound as Raymond's arm was wrenched backwards and upwards. He collapsed to the ground and was dragged under a bush.

The gun slid towards Lewis who picked it up. From around the corner, a large launch appeared, Julia standing near the stern. The gun disappeared out of Lewis's hand.

Jonathan appeared from nowhere and he was carrying the small casket.

'Raymond, is that you? Is everything okay?' a Crusader called out.

'Fine!' Jonathan shouted, hoarsely, thinking quickly. He grabbed Raymond's hat and jammed it on his head. 'But I've decided to keep these two. I think they may come in handy.'

'Don't say a word,' Jonathan whispered to Abby and Lewis, kicking the mask behind a bush.

'You have the casket?' Morris asked, leaning

out over the railing, a white bandage wrapped around his head.

Jonathan held it up in acknowledgment and waded out into the water. Lewis and Abby followed, their heads down.

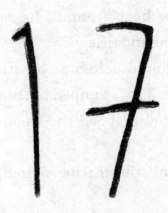

Unmasked

26 SEPTEMBER 07.39 A.M.

As the boat picked up speed, a two-way radio buzzed in the jacket of one of the men.

'Black Prince,' he said.

Lewis stared at him, quickly realising who was on the other end. How stupid! They'd left Raymond without taking his two-way. Suddenly the man stood up and took a step towards Jonathan. He was still listening to his radio.

'Turn the boat around!' he said, reaching for his automatic rifle.

Lewis glanced across at Jonathan, his face turning pale. Lewis jumped up, lunged towards Jonathan, and grabbed the wooden box away from him.

'Sit down!' the marine roared, raising his gun.

Lewis plunged his finger into the casket and vanished. The boat veered around suddenly to the right. Sensing the man was slightly off balance, Lewis kicked out at the gun, sending it flying into the water.

'Marine Crusaders, on deck now!' the man roared, swinging a punch into the air.

Lewis ducked out of the way then grabbed a life buoy and threw it at his attacker's feet. The man tripped, crashing heavily to the deck.

Suddenly six marines swarmed onto the deck, their guns snapping from person to person.

'Freeze everyone,' the marine barked, glaring at Jonathan and Abby.

But Lewis wasn't stopping. He drove

a foot firmly into the stomach of the first marine to arrive on deck, catching him by surprise. The marine stumbled backwards and overboard into the river. Then suddenly, from above the cabin trunk came a burst of gunfire. Two more marines toppled over the edge and into the water.

Lewis looked up to see Julia rolling across the roof of the boat and tumbling onto her feet on the other side.

'Take the wheel!' she yelled.

For a brief moment Lewis stood frozen, staring at Julia in total confusion. Whose side was she on?

'I'm a RODA agent. Trust me. Just do it!' she screamed.

Lewis rushed into the wheel-house and grabbed the wheel. More gunfire erupted from the deck as Jonathan and then Abby burst in.

Lewis felt Jonathan's hands take the wheel. He rushed back outside as the boat swung around again, its violent swaying causing another marine to lose his footing. Lewis moved to him quickly and, grabbing him by the collar, hauled him over the side of the boat.

'Lewis, where are you?' Julia yelled, her gun pointing at the last marine, who suddenly started firing.

Lewis ducked just as a spray of bullets whistled over his head. The marine staggered back, collapsing onto the deck. He crawled towards the Black Prince captain, who suddenly kicked out with his boot, just collecting Lewis's jaw on the way down. Lewis cried out in pain and watched in horror as the nose of the machine gun came swooping down towards him.

With one last effort, he rolled away to his left as bullets shattered the floor of the deck. Splinters of wood flew everywhere, chasing Lewis as he lunged desperately away from the frenzy of gunfire.

Then suddenly the bullets stopped as the captain collapsed to the deck.

'Let's get a move on, Mr. Ramshaw,' Julia called, jumping onto the deck and almost landing on top of Lewis. 'We've got more trouble behind.'

Lewis lifted his aching head and groaned.

Bearing down on them were three jet skis. He recognized Raymond in the blue one to the left. But there was something else in the water too.

'Crocodiles!' he shouted, then regretted it instantly. The kick to his jaw had done some damage.

'Get inside the wheel-house and let me handle this,' Julia shouted, raising her gun and firing. The first jet ski flew into the air in an explosion of water and fire as a hail of bullets shattered its petrol tank. The jet ski behind it swerved suddenly, narrowly avoiding the fireball in front. But it didn't miss a crocodile, who at that moment had decided to lift its head out of the water.

The ski slammed into the back of the crocodile's head, sending its rider flying. His head appeared for a moment before being dragged below the surface of the water.

The third jet ski pulled up suddenly,

swung around and headed off in the opposite direction. Julia lowered her gun and smiled.

'So, that was fun,' she called out, walking into the wheel-house.

Lewis found the casket and poked his finger into it, before following her in.

'Julia?' he asked, looking at her, totally perplexed.

'I think some explaining is needed,' Jonathan said, easing the throttle back and settling the boat on a steady course.

Julia looked around at the three blank faces staring at her. 'Well, my name is in fact Tamsin. Tamsin Jennings. And I can tell you that we've had our eyes on Raymond Brampton for some time.'

'*We* have?' Lewis was staring at her in wonder.

'The Agency. Enough talk for now. Let's get this boat organized.'

While Jonathan attended to Lewis's jaw, now swollen and painful, Tamsin stepped outside to clean up the mess. She tied up the captain securely to the metal railings then radioed through to base. Abby carefully guided the craft up the river, her thumping heart slowly returning to a steadier beat.

For fifteen minutes they drifted forward. Finally Abby, and then Jonathan and Lewis, reappeared inside the small cabin. Tamsin had brought along some snack bars, fruit and bottles of water. Tamsin thrust two bars into Abby's hand and took over the wheel.

'But you were Dr. Klinger?' said Abby.

'Sort of. I was chosen to step in and act the part of Deirdre Klinger.'

'You mean you're a Double Crusader?' Lewis asked.

'I was a plant. Put in by the Agency to find out whatever I could. And I can tell you I've got quite a bit to report back.'

'But I don't get it. Who attacked us back at the camp site? The first time?' Abby asked.

'That was a set-up. I had to go along with it,' Tamsin replied. 'It was Raymond Brampton's idea.'

'A daylight attack,' Jonathan said, shaking his head. 'I had my doubts about it even then.

It was so out of character with everything I knew about the Invisible Tribe.'

'Yes, and all organized by our friend, Raymond Brampton, the mask maker. Who knows how many people he has masqueraded as? He may well have hundreds of them. That ruse of his was very clever. That's when he made the swap. Raymond reappears, this time wearing the mask of Jonathan Ramshaw. His plan was always to kill Jonathan and then take over his role.'

'What?' Lewis gasped.

'Yes. He is a brilliant impersonator. Of course he might have needed to wear some padding as his body type is leaner — sorry Jonathan. He could have carried it off. Based at the school in the innocent role of a school history teacher. Wearing the perfect, seamless mask of Mr. Jonathan Ramshaw.'

'But first he had to kill me. Luckily I'd managed to crawl under some overhanging branches for cover. Brampton didn't have much time to spend looking for me. I guess he hoped the natives might kill me off instead.'

'Well, *I* couldn't find you,' Lewis said.

'I finally crept over near the boat when I thought the coast was clear. Then I heard your voices.'

'And we heard the famous scarlet macaw,' Abby grinned.

Jonathan sat down on a seat at the back of the wheel-house. Lewis sat down beside him.

'I saw her,' Lewis said softly.

Jonathan sat up suddenly. 'Amanda? You got to the tribe's village?'

Abby and Lewis told Jonathan everything that had happened since the attack at the campsite.

'And you saw her face?' Jonathan asked.

But Lewis didn't want to recall the image set in his mind. An image that he knew that would remain with him forever.

'Lewis, listen to me. Tell me again exactly what you saw.'

'I saw her face, okay?' Lewis shouted. 'She was staring up at me from the bottom of one of those poles. It was horrible. I don't want to talk about it, okay?'

But Jonathan was smiling. 'But you saw nothing else? Nothing else of her remains?'

'Um, Jonathan. Leave the poor kid be,' Tamsin said, moving towards Lewis.

'You saw nothing else because flesh in the Amazon Rainforest decomposes quickly. If there was nothing else there but bones, then there shouldn't have been a face.'

'And your point is?' Abby said, looking sickened.

'Lewis, listen to me. You didn't see your mother. You saw a Double Crusader acting as your mother. For some reason Raymond must have decided that she was too much of a risk to take with him. He probably used one of his Elite Marine Crusaders instead.'

'Which means Amanda could be at the Chalet de Sombras,' Tamsin said, slowly.

Lewis looked up, blinking through his tears.

'Are you sure?' he gasped, looking from Jonathan to Tamsin.

'No,' said Tamsin.

Abby and Lewis spent most of the seventeen hour return-flight fast asleep. They were completely oblivious to work that Tamsin had organized and was taking place as they flew high over the Pacific Ocean.

'Lewis,' Jonathan whispered, as the seatbelt sign lit up on the panel overhead. 'We're about to land.'

Lewis opened his eyes slowly and yawned. In the seat beside him, Abby smiled. The news had come through ten minutes before and she couldn't wait to break it to Lewis.

'Hey, sleepy. We're home. There's someone waiting for you,' Abby whispered gently into Lewis's ear.

'Hmmm?' he said, turning to look at her.

'Your mom.'

'Jonathan?' Lewis was wide awake now.

Jonathan nodded, his lips pressed together.

During the walk down into the customs area Lewis felt dazed. Tamsin had organized a speedy exit for them and within a few minutes, Lewis and Abby were hurried into a small waiting room.

With the casket in his hand, Jonathan strode out onto the tarmac and opened the door of a black limousine.

'Jonathan?' a woman's voice whispered from the back seat. The woman was dressed in shawls covering her entire body and scarves and wraps encircled her head.

'Hello Amanda,' he said, holding out the box. 'I am hoping this little box will be your saviour.'

'That's not your casket,' said Amanda.

'No,' Jonathan agreed. 'The one from the library was destroyed. This was given to Lewis. I believe it was a gift from the Invisible Tribe for the return of an infant he rescued. I believe this will be your saviour.'

He opened the palm of his other hand. 'It will hurt a little, but if this works the way I think it should, the pain will be worth it,' he said, taking her hand and guiding her finger into the cavity in the middle of the casket.

The woman gasped, but held her finger in place.

Gently Jonathan drew away one of the shawls

wrapped tightly around her face. 'You always had the loveliest skin, Amanda' he whispered. 'Now, there's someone else who'd like to see you. Very much.'

'Oh, Jonathan,' Amanda cried, reaching out to embrace him. 'Thank you so much,' she whispered. 'Does that mean the curse has been broken?'

'I believe so. Yours and your son's,' Jonathan said, softly.

Jonathan returned to the others in the waiting room and asked for Lewis's patience. Abby grabbed her friend's hand and held on tightly.

'Your mother just needs a little time,' said Jonathan.

Finally, a suited man came to the door and said, 'Lewis Watt?'

'That's me,' Lewis said, jumping up out of his seat.

'Would you come with me please?'

'Well?' Jonathan said, giving Lewis a nudge.

'Aren't you coming with me?' he asked.

'No,' Jonathan replied. 'There are some

things you've just got to do on your own, Lewis. And this is one of them.'

And then Lewis ran for the door.

EPILOGUE

A raid on the Chalet de Sombras took place after an alert from Special Agent Tamsin Jennings via a satellite link. An intricate underground network of rooms and tunnels beneath the old mansion revealed the shocking truth behind Raymond Brampton's work.

Thirty-seven people, including Amanda Watt, were discovered living in a series of rooms. Although all appeared in good health, the prisoners were transported to a secret location where they are undergoing a range of health checks and interviews.

Interpol and other international authorities were alerted and raids took place in a number of countries over the next twelve to thirty-six hours.

Dr. Deirdre Klinger's refusal to co-operate with Sir Raymond resulted in her incarceration at the chalet. Although she is expected to fully recover from her ordeal, her position as principal at Bridgewater was terminated by the school board. In turn, Deputy Principal, Lionel Thompson, was promoted to the position of principal of Bridgewater College.

Light Society members on the Bridgewater School Council are still helping the police with their enquiries.

An investigation into the whereabouts of Raymond Brampton, with diplomatic co-operation between over sixty-three countries, was under way. There was a report that he was last seen alive in the Amazon rainforest.

None of the Marine Crusaders involved in the most recent expedition to South America survived the adventure.

Mrs. Belcher, after receiving a large bunch of flowers and an expensive box of chocolates, decided to completely forget the peculiar incident that took place outside her boarding house with two students and the school quad bike.

Martin Caldor, who had been on leave throughout the 'school music trip' to Brazil, returned to Bridgewater. Some days his limp is more pronounced than others. His cleaning duties were extended to include the position of personal gardener for the new principal at Bridgewater College, Lionel Thompson...